Buried Treasures
of the
Mid-Atlantic States

Books in W.C. Jameson's
Buried Treasures series:

Buried Treasures of the American Southwest
Buried Treasures of the Ozarks
Buried Treasures of Texas
Buried Treasures of the Appalachians
Buried Treasures of the South
Buried Treasures of the Rocky Mountain West
Buried Treasures of California
Buried Treasures of the Pacific Northwest
Buried Treasures of the Atlantic Coast
Buried Treasures of New England
Buried Treasures of the Great Plains

Books on audio:
Buried Treasures of the Civil War
Outlaw Treasures

Buried Treasures of the Mid-Atlantic States

Legends of Island Treasure,
Jewelry Caches, and Secret Tunnels

W.C. Jameson

August House, Inc.
ATLANTA

Published 2000 by August House Publishers, Inc.

www.augusthouse.com

Printed in the United States of America

10 9 8 7 6 5 4 3 2

LIBRARY OF CONGRESS CATALOGING-IN-PUBLICATION DATA
Jameson, W.C., 1942–
Buried treasures of the Mid-Atlantic States : legends of island treasure,
jewelry caches, and secret tunnels / W.C. Jameson.
p. cm.
Includes bibliographical references.
ISBN 978-0-87483-531-1 (paper)
1. Middle Atlantic States—Antiquities—Anecdotes—Juvenile literature.
2. Treasure-trove—Middle Atlantic States—Anecdotes—Juvenile literature.
3. Middle Atlantic States—Biography—Anecdotes—Juvenile literature.
[1. Buried treasure. 2. Middle Atlantic States—History—Anecdotes.] I. Title.
F106.J29 2000
974—dc21   00-056601

Executive editor: Liz Parkhurst
Project editor: Joy Freeman
Copy editor: Dawn Drennan
Cover design and maps: Wendell E. Hall
Editorial assistant: Matt Culhane

The paper used in this publication meets the minimum requirements
of the American National Standard for Information Sciences-
Permanence of Paper for Printed Library Materials, ANSI Z39.48-1984.

August House, Inc.
ATLANTA

Contents

Introduction   7

Delaware
Thomas Cooch's Buried Coins   15
Lost Pirate Cache in the Well   19
Captain Kidd's Millsboro Treasure   25
William Neub's Buried Pirate Treasure   30
The Buried Gold of Fat Patty Cannon   35

Maryland
The Buried Treasure Chest of Jean de Champlaigne   45
Lost British Army Payroll   51
Senator Perry's Lost Treasure   57
Maryland's Lost Silver Mine   62
Braddock Heights Jewelry Cache   68

New Jersey
Jacob Fagan's Lost Loot   75
Sea Island Treasure Cache   81
Resort Treasure   86
Treasure in the Bog   92
The Lost Silver Bars in Arthur Kill   97
Secret Tunnel Treasure   102

New York
The Incredible Dutch Schultz Treasure   *109*
Lost French Gold on Treasure Island   *114*
The Lost Indian Gold Mine   *120*
Bandit Claudius Smith's Hidden Treasures   *126*
Recluse's Lost Treasure   *131*
Grand Island Treasure Caches   *136*
The Whitehall Treasure Cache   *140*

Pennsylvania
The Kinzua Bridge Bank Robbery Cache   *147*
Tons of Lost Silver Ingots   *152*
The Cursed Treasure of Bowman Hill   *157*
The Doane Gang Treasure   *162*
Dabold Hare's Lost Treasure of Gold Coins   *169*
Lost French Gold Cache in Potter County   *173*
Susquehanna Indian Silver Mine   *178*

Glossary   *183*

References   *187*

Introduction

The Mid-Atlantic States are among America's richest in terms of history, culture, legend, and lore.

Comprised of Delaware, Maryland, New Jersey, New York, and Pennsylvania, the Mid-Atlantic States are bounded on the north by Canada, on the east by the New England States and the Atlantic Ocean, on the south by Maryland and West Virginia, and on the west by Ohio.

In this setting, the Mid-Atlantic States served as a stage for a number of important episodes of early American settlement, Indian wars, the American Revolution, and the evolution of business and industry. In addition, the political and financial control of the westward expansion rested here.

At one time during the embryonic stage of the nation's settlement, these Mid-Atlantic States were considered "frontier," an unknown realm rumored to be rich in natural resources and opportunities related to trapping, hunting, farming, timber, and mineral extraction. From this region also came intriguing tales of treasure—treasure in the form of lost mines and buried loot, some treasure known only to the Indians, other treasure cached by early trappers and hunters, and still others lost or hidden by early settlers and soldiers.

The lure of opportunity and wealth in the Mid-Atlantic States—whether from business enterprises or the search for lost treasure—eventually proved to be great, and scant decades following the settlement of the coast, enterprising

Americans began moving into the unexplored regions of the Mid-Atlantic Appalachians.

Physical Landscape

The physical environment of the Mid-Atlantic States ranges from coastline to rugged mountain interiors.

The low-lying and relatively narrow easternmost part of the region facing the Atlantic Ocean is called the Coastal Plain. The irregular shoreline where the coast meets the ocean is cut by the deep indentations of Delaware Bay and Chesapeake Bay. A sandy and generally infertile area, this region is known as the pine barrens. Sand bars and lagoons extend from Cape Hatteras southward to the New York harbor.

A short distance landward, the Coastal Plain grades into the Piedmont, or foothills, region of the Appalachian Mountains. Here is also found the Fall Line, that point on the landscape where streams flowing out of the mountains meet the level plains. Here, where the gradient is gentler, the rivers are wider and largely navigable.

Not only was the Fall Line the headmost part of the navigable portion of a stream, it was also an important source of water power and served as a location for important settlements such as Trenton, New Jersey; Philadelphia, Pennsylvania; Wilmington, Delaware; and Baltimore, Maryland.

Northwestward from the Fall Line, the Appalachian ridges, valleys, and plateaus dominate the remainder of this scenic region. Though the climate throughout the area is favorable to farming, good soil occurs only in limited areas.

While agriculture is practiced in places, the most successful resource-based industrial activities found in this region of the country include the extensive mining of iron ore and coal as well as the production of steel. For well over two hundred years, timber has been associated with the Mid-Atlantic States.

Nature has had a strong hand in shaping the physical environments of the Mid-Atlantic States, and many of the current landscape features and configurations found here have resulted from eons of erosion and deposition from glaciers and flowing water.

Cultural Landscape

The cultural landscape of the Mid-Atlantic States is like the physical landscape in that it is quite varied. This area represents a true melting pot, a grand collection of Americans of diverse ethnic backgrounds. The greatest percentage of early immigrant settlers who moved into this area came from Europe—primarily English, Irish, Scotch, Dutch, Germans, and Swedes. On arriving, these newcomers often encountered various tribes of Indians already living in the region. Though separated in Europe by boundaries and politics, many of the newcomers found themselves now living side by side in America, interacting with one another and exchanging information, ideas, and folkways.

Treasure!

The mix of cultures residing together in the Mid-Atlantic States invariably gave rise to a number of folkways and folklore indigenous to the region. The roots of such lore, of course, came from Europe and the local Indian tribes, but the foodways, health practices, songs and music, and folktales eventually took on a character unique to the region, strongly flavored by the environment and the folk.

Among the many kinds of folktales to emanate from this region are fascinating stories of lost mines and buried treasures. A few of these tales originated with the Indians, some are associated with activities related to the American Revolution, some came from trappers and settlers, and others from early day outlaws.

Unlike other types of folktales, the stories and legends of lost and buried treasures of the Mid-Atlantic States remained largely uncollected and unpublished for generations. Written records of these tales were occasionally encountered in family histories, diaries, and journals, but the stories remained scattered, and many have been lost or forgotten. A number of the tales were passed down in the oral tradition and known only to a few of the older residents of the region.

This book represents an attempt to collect and present many such tales. Long days of searching through libraries in the region often yielded pertinent tales. Sometimes the stories were found in old county or state histories, occasionally in the written reminiscences of early settlers, and once in a while in an old diary or journal.

Countless meetings with members of historical societies and museum personnel resulted in the acquisition of names of a few old-timers who could relate some of the old stories. Hours of interviews with men who have searched for the lost and buried treasures, along with the descendants of those who may have actually buried some, generated more stories and filled in the gaps on others.

In a sense, these stories collected and presented herein represent another kind of treasure of the Mid-Atlantic States, a folkloric treasure that, like buried gold coins and bars of gold and silver, might have been eternally lost had not the time and effort been made to collect and preserve them.

The real treasure of the Mid-Atlantic States, however, may be the people themselves. Today's residents, many of whom are descended from the hardy stock who originally came to the region to carve out a new life, offer a precious wealth of another kind—they are friendly, open, hard-working, kind, helpful, and caring.

The quest for lost mines and buried treasures led to the discovery and meeting of many of these folk and the sharing of their collective memories and interests as they relate to the history, culture, and folklore of the area. Though much of the Mid-Atlantic region is urbanized, a significant percentage of it is still remote, and the exploration of many of these out-of-the-way valleys and hillsides in search of the tales and those who could tell them added elements of excitement, discovery, and satisfaction to the search, the quest.

Herein are presented some of the results of the quest—the stories of lost gold, silver, and jewels, of the drama of search and discovery, of the heartbreak of loss.

These stories are also about the people, their hopes, their dreams, and their adventures.

Delaware

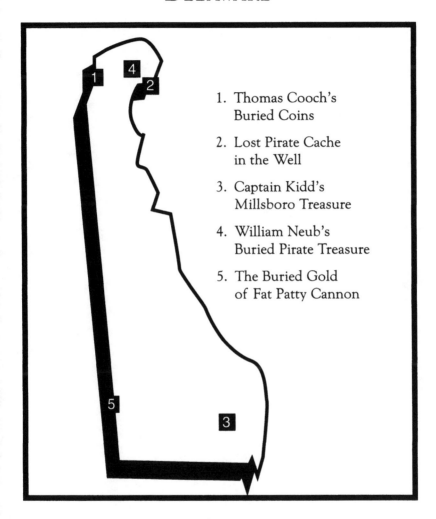

1. Thomas Cooch's
   Buried Coins

2. Lost Pirate Cache
   in the Well

3. Captain Kidd's
   Millsboro Treasure

4. William Neub's
   Buried Pirate Treasure

5. The Buried Gold
   of Fat Patty Cannon

Thomas Cooch's Buried Coins

Not far from the town of Newark in northern Delaware, Thomas Cooch, anticipating a raid by British soldiers in 1777, buried a small fortune in gold and silver coins in the woods near his gristmill. As a result of the growing war, Cooch and his family were forced to flee from the area. On returning a few years later to retrieve his money, he was unable to relocate the cache.

It is still there today, somewhere in the woods not far from the site of the old gristmill.

* * *

Thomas Cooch earned a comfortable living operating a gristmill at a northern Delaware location known at the time as Purgatory Woods. The mill was a short distance from the town of Newark, not far from White Clay Creek. Local farmers kept Cooch busy grinding their grain into flour, and the mill operator, along with his wife and daughter, often enjoyed the visits with customers and suppliers from the area.

Life was generally good for the Cooch family and their neighbors until the war broke out. The continued presence of British troops made Delaware citizens nervous, and occasional skirmishes in the area kept Thomas Cooch ever on the alert.

One afternoon during the spring of 1777, a rider warned miller Cooch that a large contingent of British troops was heading toward Purgatory Woods. Unlike previous visits from the British into the region, according to the rider, this one appeared to be oriented toward burning and looting homesteads and towns along the way.

Fearing for the safety of his family, Cooch alerted his wife and daughter of the impending danger, and together they prepared to flee the area before the arrival of the soldiers. While the women packed belongings, Cooch gathered up his life savings in gold and silver coins and placed them in a large, two-gallon wooden bowl, the coins completely filling the receptacle. After carrying the heavy load into the woods a short distance from the gristmill, Cooch excavated a shallow hole and buried his fortune.

About two hours later, after loading as many of their belongings as they could fit into their wagon, the Cooches departed for the relative safety of Pennsylvania, where they intended to stay with relatives until the hostilities subsided.

When they arrived at the gristmill several hours later, the British soldiers immediately ransacked it and burnt it to the ground. In their carelessness, the soldiers allowed the fire to spread into the surrounding woods, and by the time the raiders continued on with their march, much of the valley was ablaze.

When the Revolutionary War finally drew to a close, Thomas Cooch decided to return to his Delaware property with the intention of taking up his milling business once again. On arriving, however, he was utterly dismayed at what he found: all that remained of the gristmill was the rock foundation and a few charred timbers. The woods for miles around were scorched, and very few trees were left standing.

After surveying the damage, Thomas Cooch decided to try to find his cache of gold and silver coins, for the money would be necessary to rebuild his business enterprise.

Uncertain which direction from the gristmill he traveled when he hid the bowl filled with coins, he wandered about the area trying to find some kind of landmark. From time to time, he would stop and dig into the ground but found nothing. He was completely disoriented and frustrated and unable to locate his cache.

By sundown, Thomas Cooch realized he would likely never find the buried coins. Disheartened, he and his family climbed back into the wagon and drove into Newark, where they rented a room at an inn for several days. While his wife and daughter remained in town, Cooch returned to the area of the gristmill each day to continue the search for his money. Finally, following one failure after another, Cooch gave up, retrieved his family, and returned to Pennsylvania. He never returned to Purgatory Woods again.

As the years went by, the story of Thomas Cooch's buried coins spread throughout the northern Delaware and southeastern Pennsylvania countryside. Hopeful treasure hunters came to the burned-out woods in hopes of finding the coin cache.

During the two centuries that have passed since Cooch buried his small fortune, the wooden bowl in which the coins were placed has likely rotted away, leaving the coins lying free in the soil. Since Cooch admitted to burying the cache only a few inches in the ground, it is likely that some chance erosional event would uncover them.

This may be exactly what happened during the summer of 1952, when a five-year-old girl found a fistful of gold and silver coins near the site of Cooch's old gristmill.

The child was the daughter of man who, along with several friends, came to Purgatory Woods to search for Revolutionary War artifacts. Purgatory Woods was a popular site for artifact hunters, and collectors and hobbyists came from as far away as Ohio to look for military buttons and eighteenth century saddle fittings. After spending about three hours in the woods and finding nothing, the relic hunters were taking lunch in a shady grove when the girl approached the group and showed them the coins. Each bore mint dates between 1771 and 1775 and were covered with a dark residue. The girl was asked to lead them back to the place where she found the coins, but once in the woods, she became disoriented and was unable to retrace her steps. Though the party searched for the rest of the day, no coins were found.

On at least two other occasions, gold and silver coins bearing 1770s mint dates were found near the old gristmill. In both cases, the finders were unaware of the story of Cooch's lost cache and did not think to look for more.

From all the available evidence, it seems likely that most of Thomas Cooch's gold and silver coins are still lost somewhere in Purgatory Woods, lying at or very near the surface.

Lost Pirate Cache in the Well

The state of Delaware is seldom associated with pirates and piracy, but what may be one of the largest pirate caches in North America is believed to be hidden in a old well in the town of New Castle.

Seeking refuge from pursuing governments, a band of pirates, under the command of three ruthless and blood-thirsty captains, fled from their Madagascar hideout with a shipload of treasure. Eventually, following a long voyage across the Atlantic Ocean, they landed in New Castle, Delaware. Here, the three leaders assumed the roles of honest businessmen and soon were regarded as respectable members of the community.

In order to hide their impressive accumulation of pirate loot, the three newcomers hired a local laborer to construct a secret chamber in a well. Into this large room they stashed gold and silver ingots and coins, along with chests filled with jewelry and precious stones.

After living in New Castle for several years, the three pirate captains were eventually recognized and arrested. While awaiting trial, they escaped, stole a vessel tied up at the New Castle dock, and sailed away into the Atlantic, never to be seen again.

Many years after the escape of the pirates, the accidental discovery of a journal revealed the existence of the secret treasure-filled chamber in the well. Unfortunately, the old well had been filled in, and its location remains one of the greatest mysteries in the Mid-Atlantic States.

* * *

During the 1820s, a large band of pirates with a sizeable fleet ruled the Indian Ocean from Africa's east coast to the island of Sumatra. This feared army of brigands terrorized ships and coastal communities alike. Time and again, merchant ships carrying gold, silver, jewelry, precious stones, valuable spices, and other trade goods were attacked. After loading the valuable cargo into the hold of the pirate vessels, the crews of the merchant ships were invariably slaughtered and the vessels sunk. In a few short years, the pirates had amassed an incredible fortune that they kept hidden and under heavy guard on the island of Madagascar. Despite several efforts to storm the pirates' stronghold, the well-defended fortification remained under the complete control of the brigands.

Eventually, the governments of England, Spain, and Holland, tired of enduring the huge losses to the pirates, combined forces to patrol the Indian Ocean in the hope of overtaking the plunderers. The pirates were to be shown no mercy: those not killed during an encounter were to be hanged at the first opportunity. Learning of the combined efforts of the three nations, the three bold commanders of the large pirate force decided to abandon the area and flee to the safety of the United States. Loading their fortunes onto three ships, they set sail for the Atlantic Coast and weeks later arrived at New Castle in the upper reaches of Delaware Bay where the Delaware River enters.

The crewmen and sailors were paid off and sent on their way, and the quiet riverside community enthusiastically welcomed the three newcomers, little realizing they were among the most notorious and ruthless pirates ever to sail the Indian Ocean. The pirate captains posed as wealthy investors from England with interests in establishing an export business in

New Castle. Shortly after arriving, each of them contracted to have a fine home constructed not far from the riverfront. On the property of one of the houses, a large well was dug. The well-digger, a local man, was a bit surprised when provided his instructions—he was to excavate a well twice as wide as a conventional one, with a chamber dug into one side just above the water level. The well-digger also was told not to mention a word to anyone about the project. If he did, cautioned one of his employers, he would be killed.

True to his word, the well-digger, whose name was Blake, never told a soul about his strange assignment. He did, however, keep a journal, and each night on returning to his room in New Castle, Blake recorded his progress on the well and the mysterious chamber.

Blake struck water at twenty-eight feet. At approximately twenty-two feet below the surface, the digger undertook the excavation of a lateral passageway. A doorway about two-and-a-half feet high and two feet wide opened into a similar-sized shaft that, in turn, led to a twenty- by twenty-foot chamber with a seven-foot ceiling. The chamber was fortified with stout wooden beams. Finally, a door and frame made of cast iron were fashioned at a local blacksmith shop and positioned at the entrance to the chamber and cemented into the rocks lining the well. The door was fitted with a heavy lock.

One evening a few days after the iron door was installed, Blake was out for a walk and happened to pass near the new well. As he stood some distance away, hidden by some hedges, he watched his employers carry objects from their new homes and lower them into the well. For several hours they worked, finally halting their efforts only two hours before dawn. Among the objects Blake saw lowered into the well were several heavy wooden chests.

When the well-digger returned to his dwelling, he recorded his observations in his journal, ate a small breakfast, and, as the sun was already rising, returned to the well to complete some stonework.

It was the last time anyone ever saw him.

For nearly three years the newcomers lived quietly in New Castle. In spite of their promises to establish a business, no apparent effort was made to do so. Neighbors also noted that, although a great deal of labor and expense went into the construction of the new well, no one was ever seen drawing water from it. And the strange disappearance of the old well-digger remained a mystery.

One day, an American naval vessel sailed up to the New Castle dock, and a number of uniformed officers disembarked and sought an audience with local authorities. Following a full afternoon of discussion, the officers, accompanied by New Castle officials and a contingent of armed sailors, went to the homes of each of the mysterious businessmen and arrested them. Moments after they were placed in the New Castle jail, word spread through town that the men were pirates and were wanted by the governments of several foreign countries.

Charged with a variety of offenses, including murder, robbery, kidnapping, and piracy, the three brigands were kept in the New Castle jail to await deportation. Three days after their incarceration, the pirates subdued a jailer, took his keys, and escaped. In the dark of night, they fled to the New Castle dock, where they stole a small schooner and sailed away. When the jailbreak was reported the next morning, several ships were sent out in pursuit of the pirates, but they were never seen. It was believed they fled to South America.

Because of the suddenness of their arrest and the haste

with which they fled Delaware, the pirates had no opportunity to carry away any of their treasure with them. In fact, no one was ever aware that such a treasure existed until fifty years later when the old well-digger's journal was discovered. When Blake failed to show up at his rented room, his landlady summoned the well-digger's son, who lived a short distance upriver in Wilmington. When the son arrived by wagon several days later, the landlady had the old man's belongings waiting for him—all packed into a single trunk. After a cursory look through the trunk, the son thanked the woman, loaded it into the wagon, and returned to Wilmington.

On arriving back at his home in Wilmington, the son placed his father's trunk in the attic, and it was soon forgotten. Thirty years later, he passed away, and his son, the well-digger's grandson, moved into the house with his wife and two-year-old son.

When the boy was thirteen, he was exploring the attic of the house and found the old, dust-covered trunk. When asked what it contained, his father could not tell him for he had never seen it before. Together, the two carried the trunk from the attic to the den and opened it.

Inside were a few articles of clothing, a pair of leather work gloves, some coins, and a small carving of a whale in ivory. At the bottom of the trunk was a journal, its pages yellowed and brittle with age. Father and son examined the journal for several minutes, reading aloud a few of the entries in the smooth script of their ancestor. Most of the notes related to well-digging jobs, conversations with friends, activities at the taverns, and the subjects of a number of church sermons. Before they were well into the journal, the pair was called to supper. They replaced the journal in the trunk, and later that evening they returned it to the attic.

Two more years passed, and the boy became interested in the trunk once again. This time, as he was perusing the journal, he encountered a series of entries describing the well and the secret chamber. After reading the journal closely, the boy excitedly summoned his father, and together they learned about the curious project of nearly fifty years earlier, along with the clandestine activities of the strange New Castle residents for whom the well-digger worked.

It was apparent to the father and son that the men who hired the well-digger were intent on hiding a large number of valuable objects in the chamber. When opportunity permitted, the two traveled to New Castle to try to locate information pertinent to the old journal. After three days of examining documents at City Hall and the library, they learned of the mysterious disappearance of their ancestor and the arrest and escape of the pirates.

The two decided to try to determine the location of the old well containing the treasure-filled chamber. After examining a number of old town plats, they narrowed their search to a piece of property not far from the old New Castle jail. They were certain they had located the exact lot on which the well had been dug, but no sign of one could be found anywhere. Frustrated, they returned to Wilmington.

Continued research during subsequent weeks revealed the fact that, because of an outbreak of some unidentified waterborne disease that infected the New Castle residents during the 1880s, many of the town's wells were filled in.

Somewhere within the city limits of New Castle, approximately twenty-two feet beneath the surface near an old filled-in well, lies a twenty- by twenty-foot chamber filled with what may be one of the largest pirate treasures ever hidden on the North American continent.

Captain Kidd's
Millsboro Treasure

The notorious pirate Captain William Kidd is known to have buried stolen booty up and down much of the east coast of the United States. Over the years, Kidd returned for and recovered much of his treasure, but according to researchers, a great deal of it remains buried and lost. One such cache is believed to exist not far from Indian River Bay near the Sussex County town of Millsboro, a cache consisting of several chests filled with gold, jewels, precious stones, and uncut diamonds.

* * *

During 1699, Captain Kidd, one of the most widely known and successful pirates of all time, guided his vessel into the quiet waters of Indian River Bay in southern Delaware. The ship, heavy with captured booty, was riding low, and Kidd was concerned about becoming stuck in the shallow waters.

For the past several weeks, Kidd had buried captured treasure at several locations along the Atlantic Coast, treasures he intended to return for when he was ready to retire from piracy.

Presently, the sailor perched at the end of the bow signaled to Kidd that they were very close to the bottom. Kidd ordered the anchor dropped, and moments later crewmen were busy loading heavy wooden chests from the ship into one of the longboats. After the chests were placed in the craft, a cannonball, taken from one of the nearby gun placements, was lowered into the boat and laid between two chests. Finally, Kidd climbed into the boat and directed the

25

oarsmen to land it on a nearby southern shore.

The pirate crewmen alternately carried and dragged the heavy chests up the bank to a location near a single large oak tree. Each trunk was unlocked and opened, and, as two men undertook the excavation of a deep hole, Captain Kidd briefly examined the contents of each. One contained gold coins taken from a raid on a British merchant vessel, another contained gold from China, a third was filled with jewelry and precious stones such as sapphires, emeralds, and rubies, and the last was filled nearly to the top with uncut diamonds. After each trunk was closed and locked, Kidd watched as they were lowered into the six-foot-deep hole.

Once the hole was covered, Kidd carved a diamond-shaped symbol into the trunk of the oak tree. The cannonball, carried to the location by Kidd, was placed directly over the newly buried cache. This done, Kidd and his crewmen returned to the ship.

Several weeks later, Captain Kidd was captured and placed in the Boston jail. Later tried for piracy, he was executed in 1701. The pirate was never able to return to Indian River Bay to retrieve his buried treasure-filled chests.

* * *

One afternoon during June 1932, a black Ford panel truck pulled to a stop at Millsboro's only gas station. While young Jimmy Butler, the son of the owner, filled the gas tank, the driver and passenger inquired about lodging. Butler told them his mother often rented a spare room to travelers, and he gave them directions to his house.

The following morning, the two travelers returned to the gas station and sought an audience with young Butler. For several minutes, they asked the youth about certain landmarks and directions. Every now and then, one of the men

26

would unroll a large map and refer to something on it.

Specifically, the newcomers wished to know the location of a large oak tree located near the southern shore of the upper reaches of Indian River Bay. Butler was familiar with the tree, had played near it many times, and told the men he would lead them directly to it.

The next day was Butler's day off, and around nine o'clock he departed with the two men toward the bay. As the driver steered the vehicle out of town, Butler directed him along a series of bumpy dirt roads. About one-half hour later they finally arrived at a broad meadow, at the far end of which stood a large, impressive oak tree. Toward this the driver steered the truck.

The oak tree grew at the head of a low bank that graded gently toward the bay, about fifty yards away. The two men climbed out of the truck and walked quickly toward the tree. As Butler remained near the truck, the men circled the tree as if searching for something. Presently, one of them cried out that he had found it, and when Butler approached, he saw them pointing to an odd mark on the trunk. About breast high on the tree, Butler discerned a diamond-shaped figure that had apparently been slashed into the tree many years ago. The cut had been partially covered by new bark growth, but it was clear it had been man-made.

One of the men had been carrying the same rolled up map Butler had seen earlier, and now he spread it out on the ground near the bole of the tree. Butler could see that the map was very old and made from some kind of heavy parchment. As Butler watched, the men pointed to features on the map and coordinated them with existing landmarks. Finally, Butler asked if it was a treasure map.

The two men explained that it was and that it had been

found in a trunk in North Carolina several years earlier. The mapmaker was one of the crewmen who accompanied Kidd to the site of the Indian River Bay treasure cache. As young Butler stood spellbound, they related the story of the pirate Captain Kidd burying several chests filled with treasure near the tree. They also told the boy that if he would keep their activities secret, they would cut him in for a share of the treasure. Returning to the map, one of the men said the cache was marked by a cannonball. Butler told them that a cannonball was, in fact, discovered near this site several years earlier. The finder carried it home and later donated it to a museum in Washington, D.C.

Frustrated at the loss of the important marker, the men began pacing off distances from the tree. After nearly an hour, they agreed on one particular location and began digging. Around three o'clock in the afternoon, they had excavated to seven feet when they decided they had calculated wrong.

Every day for the next two weeks, the two men and Butler returned to the large oak tree. After checking the map and calculating distances and directions, they would decide on a new location and dig yet another hole. Each time, they failed to locate any treasure.

About three days after excavating the first hole, the two treasure hunters finally located the man who had found the cannonball. Since the discovery had taken place years earlier, the finder could not recall where it was found relative to distance and direction from the old oak. Finally, the two men gave up their search and departed Millsboro. They were never seen again.

After the men left, young Butler often returned to the oak tree. Fascinated with the tale of Captain Kidd's treasure, he found himself imbued with the idea of locating it. On numerous occasions he dug holes near the tree in search of the fabulous cache but found nothing. After several failures, Butler eventually grew frustrated and ceased his efforts to locate the treasure.

Today, the large oak tree that grew near the spot where Captain Kidd buried well over a million dollars' worth of treasure is gone. Having succumbed to age, it was removed many years ago. In Millsboro, no one recalls exactly where it stood, and confusion reigns relative to the suspected location of Captain Kidd's Indian River Bay treasure.

At this writing, a team of electronics experts are experimenting with a state-of-the-art metal detector capable of picking up signals up to eight feet deep. They plan to travel to Millsboro to search for Kidd's treasure. And they are convinced they will find it.

William Neub's
Buried Pirate Treasure

During the mid-1720s, the notorious pirate William Neub decided to retire from a long career of brigandage and settle down to a quiet life where no one knew him. Neub purchased a farm between New Castle and Newark and moved his impressive fortune in gold, jewels, and precious stones to the site, a fortune gleaned from years of piracy and estimated to be worth millions. A suspicious neighbor, knowing that New Castle authorities were looking for Neub, reported his presence in Delaware. When the former pirate learned he was about to be arrested, he quickly buried his wealth on his farm and marked the location by scratching the image of an anchor and chain on a nearby rock. The end of the chain pointed directly to the treasure trove.

Pirate Neub fled from the area intending to return someday for his treasure, but he was never seen again in the northern Delaware location. The search for the elusive anchor and chain carving has continued for over 250 years; it has been found on at least two occasions.

The treasure, however, remains lost.

* * *

After more than twenty years of successful piracy in the Indian and Atlantic Oceans, as well as the Caribbean Sea, freebooter William Neub was gradually coming to the conclusion that he was growing too old for the dangers of continuous raiding and fighting. With a mane of gray hair, the so-called Scourge of the Atlantic found himself slowing down as he approached his fiftieth birthday, and his enthusiasm for piracy was wearing thin. His three dozen scars, along with over one dozen healed broken bones, were causing him great pain on cold mornings. Furthermore, pursuit from British and American gunships was growing more frequent, making successful raids of merchant vessels and coastal communities increasingly difficult.

Neub finally announced to his pirate crew that he was retiring. After dividing the spoils of recent raids, Neub sailed up Delaware Bay to New Castle. Here, he turned the ship over to his first mate and had his belongings, along with two wooden chests filled with treasure, deposited on the New Castle dock.

Several weeks later, Neub, passing himself off as a cattleman, purchased a farm in the fertile lands between New Castle and Newark. For nearly eighteen months, Neub lived a quiet and peaceful life. He rarely encountered neighbors, and on the few occasions he ventured into New Castle to purchase supplies, he tarried only long enough to quaff an ale or two at a local tavern before returning home.

With each passing month, Neub's neighbors grew increasingly suspicious of the newcomer. Since moving onto his farm, Neub had neither stocked it with cattle nor tilled any of the land. In spite of having no apparent source of income, Neub always seemed to have plenty of money.

Eventually, one of Neub's neighbors learned of the newcomer's pirate background. During a visit to New Castle, the neighbor discovered that authorities were offering rewards for information relative to the locations of a number of pirates who committed depredations along the Atlantic Coast during the previous ten years. Neub was one of them.

When the authorities learned that Neub was living close by, they began to make plans to capture and arrest him. Three days after being informed of Neub's whereabouts, a New Castle constable organized a contingent of some fifteen armed men, who rode out to the ex-pirate's farm.

Meanwhile, the man who identified Neub to the authorities told several area residents what he had done. One of them, a man who had himself spent a portion of his life aboard pirate vessels, immediately rode to Neub's farm to warn him. Realizing he had only a very short time to escape, Neub packed a few belongings and filled his pockets with gold coins. He then dragged his treasure-filled chests some distance from his house and quickly buried them. On a nearby rock, Neub carved the image of an anchor and chain, with the end of the chain pointing in the direction of the buried cache. Following this, Neub fled westward into Maryland and was never seen again.

* * *

In 1842, a man who identified himself only as Thomas arrived at Newark inquiring about the old Neub farm. Since more than a century had elapsed since the pirate fled from Delaware, no one was familiar with the name. After several days of searching through old courthouse records, however, Thomas eventually found the information he desired.

Thomas, who rarely conversed with any of the Newark townspeople, made several trips from his rented room to the old Neub property. Eventually, a Newark constable became suspicious and confronted the stranger. Realizing he would be unable to continue unless he cooperated with the constable, Thomas confessed that he was searching for the lost treasure of one Captain William Neub, the pirate. When the constable expressed doubts, Thomas unrolled an old, yellowed parchment. According to Thomas, the map was drawn by William Neub himself. On examining it, the constable could identify several familiar landmarks. On the section of the map that contained an outline of the old Neub property, he noted an illustration of an anchor and chain. Thomas explained that Neub had carved the image into a rock not far from where he buried the treasure and that the chain pointed to the location of the cache.

With the help of the constable, Thomas returned often to the Neub farm, but after nearly eight months of continuous searching for the buried treasure cache, he was unable to find it. Discouraged, he finally left Newark.

* * *

In 1888, two strangers arrived at Newark and soon were observed exploring around what was once the property of William Neub. After receiving several complaints from area residents, law officers arrested the two men for trespassing. After being interrogated for two hours, they finally admitted they were searching for a cache of buried pirate treasure. As proof, they unrolled a large map they had in their possession and showed it to the policemen. From the description of the map, it was very likely the same one brought to Newark by the man named Thomas more than four decades earlier. The two newcomers claimed they purchased the map at an estate auction.

Arrangements were made to allow the two strangers to continue their search for the cache. After several weeks of failure, they decided to seek information from several area residents, asking each of them if he had ever seen a rock with the image of an anchor and chain scratched onto the surface. No one admitted to seeing such a rock until an elderly resident named Bradley was interviewed. Bradley claimed he had seen such a rock on numerous occasions while rabbit hunting. He described it much as it was identified on the old map.

With the help of Bradley, the two newcomers conducted several searches on the old Neub property, but they were never able to find the rock.

* * *

During the 1970s, a man named Gerard arrived at Newark with yet another map purporting to show the location of the buried pirate treasure. Instead of searching for the rock with the anchor and chain inscription himself, Gerard placed an ad in the local newspaper requesting information on such a stone.

Almost immediately, he received a visit from a man named Benson who said he once had worked with a road-construction crew that performed maintenance on nearby Highway 40, a well-traveled route that bisects northern Delaware. According to Benson, a large rock bearing the image of a ship's anchor and accompanying chain was pushed aside by a bulldozer several years earlier during some routine road work. The rock was moved approximately fifty feet from its original location and had fractured into several pieces during the process.

Since pirate Neub buried his treasure-filled chests in haste, they likely lay close to the surface, close enough that the contents would surely trigger a response from a sensitive metal detector. It is also likely, according to Benson, that Captain William Neub's treasure may have been partially covered by a portion of Highway 40.

The Buried Gold of
Fat Patty Cannon

Patty Cannon, known to her Reliance neighbors as Fat Patty, owned and operated a tavern near the Delaware-Maryland line during the early 1800s. Aided by her husband and son-in-law, Fat Patty Cannon orchestrated a number of robberies and killings of her customers over several years. In addition to murder, Fat Patty operated a slave ring that did a healthy business stealing and selling slaves. It is estimated that, over a period of ten years, Fat Patty and her gang robbed and murdered at least thirty-seven businessmen. Fat Patty buried between $75,000 and $150,000 in gold coins at several secret locations near her tavern. Before Fat Patty could spend any of the buried wealth, she, along with her son-in-law, was arrested. While awaiting trial, both committed suicide. With the death of Fat Patty Cannon went the knowledge of the location of the buried gold caches.

* * *

Patty Cannon migrated from Canada to Delaware when she was only sixteen years old. She remained secretive about her past, and all that is known about her is that she was the daughter of gypsies. While struggling to make a living in Delaware, Patty sometimes worked as a barmaid and other times as a cleaning lady. While serving ale to travelers one night in a Dover brothel, she became aware of the relatively large sums of money earned by the prostitutes—considerably more than she made as a barmaid. The following week, Patty traded in her apron for some fancy clothes, and for the next few years she practiced her new trade and saved her money, intending someday to open a bordello of her own.

The years were not kind to Patty Cannon. With a large frame and a healthy appetite, she had a tendency to put on weight. By the time she was twenty-four, she had grown to 260 pounds. Gradually, her customers moved on to other girls, and Patty soon found herself with nothing but her savings.

Despite her efforts to save money, Patty had not been able to accumulate quite enough to purchase a brothel and stock it with classy girls. Instead, she settled for a two-story log tavern in the town of Reliance on the Delaware-Maryland border. Here she sold ale and an occasional meal to businessmen and other travelers and sometimes rented out a room.

Patty, never particularly friendly with her neighbors to begin with, had grown surly with age and increasingly hard to get along with. In time, Reliance citizens generally shunned her and avoided her place of business in favor of others. They also began referring to her as Fat Patty, a nickname she carried for the rest of her life.

In spite of Patty's deteriorating looks and abrasive personality, she found favor with one Jesse Carver, a widower. Carver was a local drunk who seldom held a job for more than one week at a time, but Patty had gone a long time without having a man around. Once wed, Patty put Carver to work doing chores around the tavern and the grounds.

The family grew when Joe Johnson, Jesse's son-in-law, came to live with them. Both men, tall and strapping, were completely cowed by the bullying Patty. Not only was she strong as a bull, she has been described in historical documents as "of a fierce temperament and homicidal." More than once, Patty had hoisted an unruly tavern patron over her shoulder and thrown him out the door.

As Fat Patty's tavern business decreased, she looked for other ways to make money. Eventually, she settled upon the idea of selling slaves to area farmers. With the help of Carver and Johnson, Fat Patty would travel to Virginia, steal slaves from wealthy landowners, carry them back to Delaware and Maryland, and sell them to the highest bidders. So profitable was this new venture that Fat Patty made an incredible $25,000 in gold coins in the first year, an enormous sum for 1819.

When Fat Patty, Carver, and Johnson returned to Reliance with captured slaves, they would house them on the second floor of the tavern until they could be sold in the region. From time to time, Fat Patty would carry a horsewhip to the second floor and mercilessly beat the shackled and manacled slaves.

On at least two occasions, Fat Patty, annoyed by the crying of young slave children, snatched a baby from its mother, carried it downstairs, and flung it into the fireplace.

During the summer of 1819, a well-known Virginia farmer named Edwin Ravenal arrived at Fat Patty's tavern. After introducing himself, he told Patty that, like her, he was also in the slave-trading business. He said he had a buyer who needed about one dozen slaves to work on a North Carolina plantation. The buyer, according to Ravenal, was willing to pay top dollar for good workers. With that, Ravenal jingled a heavy purse lying at bottom of his coat pocket. The sound of gold pieces immediately aroused Fat Patty's interest, as well as that of Carver and Johnson, who were sitting nearby.

Fat Patty told Ravenal they could probably do business and that she had several strong slaves for sale. She invited Ravenal to sit at a table and steered him to one near a side window. While she poured cups of rum, Fat Patty nodded to her husband and son-in-law, who quietly rose from their chairs and slipped out the back door of the tavern.

While Ravenal and Fat Patty were toasting each other and discussing business, Johnson went to a nearby shed and retrieved a heavy musket. Followed by Carver, Johnson crept around the tavern to the side window and peered in. Seated only six feet away with his back toward him was Ravenal. Quietly lifting the musket, Johnson aimed for the back of the planter's head and squeezed the trigger. Ravenal was killed instantly, and the moment he fell to the tavern floor, Fat Patty was searching though his pockets for the gold. After yanking the pouch of money from the garment, she ordered Carver and Johnson to get rid of the body.

The two men carried the limp form of Edwin Ravenal across the yard to a wagon. Though Fat Patty told them to bury the body far away and near the Nanticoke River, the two men decided instead to simply toss it into some bushes along the road. Back at the tavern, Fat Patty counted out $10,000 in gold coins.

The next day, Sussex County lawmen found Ravenal's body and set out to try to find his killer. Fat Patty Cannon, Carver, and Johnson were all questioned, but each made alibis for the other. A week later, the lawmen caught Joe Johnson riding Ravenal's horse, but the son-in-law claimed he purchased it from a man passing through the area. Though the lawmen did not have enough evidence to charge Fat Patty and the men with a crime, they nevertheless began keeping an eye on the activities in the tavern.

Over the next few years, rumors about prominent area businessmen vanishing after renting a room at Fat Patty's tavern were rampant around the Reliance area. Occasionally, law enforcement authorities would arrive at the tavern to question the proprietress, Carver, and Johnson, but each time they came away lacking sufficient justification to press charges.

For a period of about ten years, Fat Patty, always a frugal woman, accumulated several thousand dollars' worth of gold taken from her victims. While Carver and Johnson would take the dead men's horses into Virginia to sell them, Fat Patty secretly buried the money in several locations around the tavern. It has been estimated that Fat Patty Cannon buried between $75,000 and $150,000 worth of gold coins.

Finally, Fat Patty made a mistake—she fell in love with one of her potential victims! His name was Harris, and he was from the Delaware town of Staytonville, located about twenty miles northeast of Reliance. Harris had been buying and selling slaves for years, had heard about Fat Patty's lucrative operation, and decided to conduct some business with her.

As Fat Patty and Harris discussed the slave trade at the table near the side window, the smitten tavern owner waved off her husband and son-in-law, who were preparing to kill the visitor. Stunned by Fat Patty's decision, the two men watched as Harris placed a number of gold coins into Fat Patty's pudgy hands. Minutes later, the businessman was riding away with six husky slaves in tow. Before he left, Harris told Fat Patty he would return for four more slaves within two days.

Knowing that Harris had a leather purse filled with gold on his person, Carver and Johnson were dismayed that Fat Patty allowed him to ride away. Jesse Carver, however, had noticed the way Fat Patty looked at the newcomer, and he gradually worked himself into a jealous rage. Slipping away from Fat Patty and Johnson, Carver saddled a horse and rode down the trail after Harris.

Late that afternoon, Fat Patty heard someone ride up to the front of the tavern and went to see who it was. Carver dismounted and was tying his horse, along with another, to the hitching post. Fat Patty immediately recognized the extra horse as the one on which Harris had ridden away earlier in the day.

Stepping up onto the porch, Carver, grinning, held up a leather purse and shook it, jingling the gold coins inside. Fat Patty saw that the purse was the same one from which Harris extracted payment for the six slaves only a few hours earlier. When Fat Patty Cannon realized what her husband had done, she attacked him, striking him with her fists and knocking him off the porch and onto the ground. Jumping atop her husband, Fat Patty then began to beat Carver unmercifully. By the time she was finished, the unconscious man lay bleeding from several cuts on his face and head.

The next morning, Fat Patty apologized to Carver for her behavior and offered to prepare him a big breakfast of pork chops and eggs. After only a few bites, Carver grabbed at his stomach and, gasping for breath, fell to the floor. Moments later he was dead. That afternoon, after informing Johnson that she had poisoned his father-in-law, Fat Patty loaded Carver into the wagon and drove him toward the river to bury him with the others.

Meanwhile, the six manacled slaves who had left the tavern with Harris were making their way along the Federalsburg-Seaford Road when they were discovered by law enforcement authorities. After questioning the slaves, the lawmen learned about Fat Patty Cannon's illegal operation, the murder of Harris, the killings of the slave children, and enough information to link her with several more crimes.

The following morning, the lawmen arrived at the tavern and arrested Fat Patty Cannon and Joe Johnson. As the two were being questioned, Johnson, who expressed a fear of hanging, admitted his part in the numerous killings and implicated Fat Patty. He also directed the lawmen to the second floor of the tavern, where eight slaves were chained to the wall.

The following morning, the two prisoners were transported to nearby county seat of Georgetown, where they were held in jail awaiting trial for kidnapping, robbery, and murder. Two days before her trial date, Fat Patty swallowed a handful of poison she had somehow hidden in the folds of her clothes. She died within minutes.

The following day, Johnson, who told a jailer he couldn't face execution, hung himself in his jail cell.

Fat Patty Cannon's tavern stood empty, dark, and unused for the next few decades. Reliance townsfolk seldom visited the property, and many claimed they could hear the wailing of the ghosts of those killed there. In 1890, the building was torn down.

Fat Patty's property passed through several owners during the next century. From time to time, people would arrive at the site to search for the buried gold known to be cached there, but most attempts to find the gold were complete failures. In 1910, however, one lucky treasure hunter stumbled onto a cache of about one hundred coins. The coins had been placed in several small glass jars and buried only twelve feet from the old tavern location. Two more caches were found, one in 1921 and another in 1950.

Today, a two-story house sits on the exact site once occupied by Fat Patty Cannon's tavern. Now and then, treasure hunters arrive to search for the remaining caches of gold coins. Fat Patty Cannon left no journals or other information to provide clues for the locations of the caches, but most researchers contend they were buried close to the tavern.

MARYLAND

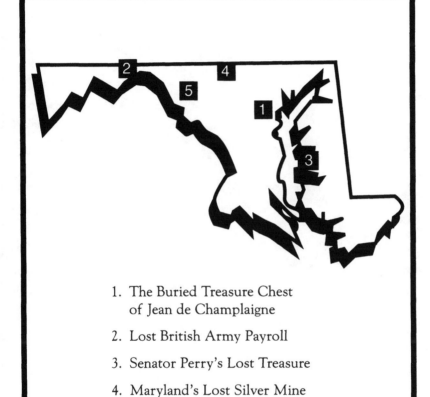

1. The Buried Treasure Chest
   of Jean de Champlaigne

2. Lost British Army Payroll

3. Senator Perry's Lost Treasure

4. Maryland's Lost Silver Mine

5. Braddock Heights Jewelry Cache

The Buried Treasure Chest of Jean de Champlaigne

When prominent French shipping company owner Jean de Champlaigne retired to his Catonsville, Maryland, property, he brought with him a fortune in gold coins. In time, de Champlaigne grew increasingly reclusive and paranoid and eventually went insane. During the final days of his life, according to his servant, the Frenchman spent most of his time counting his money.

With the help of the trusted servant, Champlaigne counted out his gold, placed it in a wooden sea chest, and buried it in an unmarked location near the house. Weeks later, Champlaigne died, and, as a result of a promise made to his employer, the servant refused to reveal the location of the buried treasure cache.

To date, the de Champlaigne treasure, believed to be worth well over a million dollars at today's gold values, has not been found.

* * *

Entrepreneur Jean de Champlaigne enjoyed a fine reputation throughout Europe's major business circles. His success at building one of the continent's largest shipping concerns earned him a place in high society throughout France, Germany, and Great Britain. De Champlaigne soon counted among his friends a number of important politicians, corporate executives, and military leaders. One of his close associates was the famous General Napoleon Bonaparte.

Unfortunately, de Champlaigne's friendship with Napoleon could not prevent the disaster that was soon to befall his shipping enterprises. As Napoleon rose to power in France, he determined it was important to destroy Great Britain's shipping and trading activities with the United States and other countries. Outraged, the United States retaliated by refusing to allow French vessels to dock at American ports. His business seriously impaired, de Champlaigne pleaded with the general to ease up on the trade restrictions. Instead, Napoleon rigidly adhered to his position and even gave orders for his navy to attack and sink any American trading vessels they encountered in the Atlantic Ocean. Angered, the Americans responded by sending armed American warships into the Atlantic to destroy French vessels. Many of the ships sunk by the American navy belonged to de Champlaigne.

At the height of the conflict, de Champlaigne, his business decimated, decided to flee France. Fearing he had made far too many enemies among the leaders of the French government, the entrepreneur hurriedly accumulated his wealth, approximately $50,000 worth of gold coins, packed his belongings, and fled to Canada. From Canada, he booked passage on a British ship and eventually arrived at Baltimore, Maryland.

De Champlaigne purchased a fine home in Catonsville, Maryland, today a suburb of Baltimore. The large house, located in the middle of twenty acres of dense woodland, served de Champlaigne well. A lifelong bachelor, the Frenchman grew increasingly reclusive with the passing years and was convinced the insular nature of his new residence protected him from the prying eyes and curious natures of his new neighbors.

De Champlaigne employed a single servant, a black man named Horace, who cooked, cleaned, and cared for the Frenchman. Horace was intensely loyal and dedicated to de Champlaigne and efficiently saw to his every personal need. Horace would occasionally take a horse-drawn wagon into town to purchase supplies, but, in spite of being asked many questions about his strange employer, he refused to discuss the matter with anyone. During the years that de Champlaigne lived at his Maryland estate, he was seen only rarely, so reclusive was his nature. In addition, he grew paranoid and confessed to Horace almost daily that he was convinced his neighbors were going to attack and burn the house and steal his gold.

According to Horace, de Champlaigne spent the last few months of his life counting his gold over and over and recalling the days when he was a successful and important businessman in France, regaling the servant with stories of big business deals, public appearances, political connections, and grand balls and parties. Horace understood little of what was said but patiently allowed the Frenchman to ramble on. Horace was aware that de Champlaigne was growing more and more demented with each passing day.

One morning, de Champlaigne asked Horace to help him pack his gold coins into a stout wooden chest. As the Frenchman counted out each piece, he handed it to the servant, who patiently placed it into the chest. When de Champlaigne was finished, the chest was nearly full and quite heavy. After it was closed and secured with a huge lock, the two men alternately carried and dragged the cumbersome chest outside and into the yard. Not far from the house, de Champlaigne instructed Horace to dig a hole. When the excavation was about three feet deep, the black man was ordered to slide the chest into the cavity and shovel the dirt back on top of it.

Under instructions from de Champlaigne, Horace smoothed

47

over the surface of the refilled hole and covered it with leaves, small branches, and other forest debris, making it appear much like any other part of the yard. After getting Horace to promise he would never reveal the location of the buried gold to anyone, de Champlaigne, laughing insanely, led the way back into the house.

Several weeks following the burial of the coin-filled chest, de Champlaigne died. According the Frenchman's will, the house and land were sold and the money given to Horace. Suddenly finding himself with more wealth than he ever imagined possible, Horace purchased a small house in Baltimore, where he lived for the next two decades.

* * *

Approximately three years after the death of de Champlaigne, two of the late businessman's nephews arrived by ship in Baltimore. The only surviving relatives of the Frenchman, the nephews possessed records that showed de Champlaigne left France with $50,000 in gold coins. On learning that the former shipping tycoon had died, the nephews, regarded as legal heirs, came to the United States to claim their inheritance.

The nephews spent three weeks in Baltimore trying to locate their uncle's attorney and the bank where he conducted his business. Since de Champlaigne availed himself of neither, the two young men remained confused and uncertain of what to do. Presently, the two learned about their uncle's trusted servant Horace, and they immediately looked him up.

In spite of pleadings, promises, and ultimately threats, Horace refused to reveal to the nephews the location of the buried chest of gold coins, saying only that it was somewhere on the property. Eventually realizing they would not learn anything from Horace, the two men went to the former de Champlaigne estate to see if they could locate the cache. After digging several holes and disturbing the new owners, the nephews were chased away from the property. A few days later they returned at night and managed to excavate several more holes before they were discovered. The third time they entered the property, they were arrested by the constable and placed in the Baltimore jail for two weeks. When they were released, the two men boarded a ship for France, never to return.

* * *

During the twenty years following the passing of de Champlaigne, rumors of his buried chest of gold coins spread throughout the Maryland and Virginia countryside. From time to time, individuals would appear at the former de Champlaigne residence to search for the treasure, but they were invariably escorted away by law enforcement authorities. Holes were sometimes dug, hollow trees were closely investigated, every crevice and opening in exposed rock was explored, and wooden planks were even removed from the house, but no treasure was ever found.

Horace eventually grew old and enfeebled, unable to manage the house in which he lived. Nearly helpless, he was eventually invited to move in with a niece. Now in his eighties, the former servant occasionally submitted to interviews and questions about de Champlaigne's buried treasure.

During one such interview, Horace stated that he didn't think it would matter any longer if he revealed the location of the coin-filled chest. Assisted by his niece and a professional treasure hunter from New York City, Horace returned to the de Champlaigne estate for the first time since he left it decades earlier.

Standing in front of the house, Horace, clearly confused, looked around the yard as if he were lost. He told the man from New York City that everything appeared to be different, that the house was changed, and that a number of the trees in the yard had been cut down.

Horace related that, after he and de Champlaigne dragged the heavy treasure chest out of the house and down the steps of the wooden porch, they stopped to rest. Renewing their efforts, the two men pulled and pushed the heavy wooden container a short distance across a portion of the front yard but finally halted when they grew too tired to transport it any farther. "At that spot," said Horace, "Mister de Champlaigne told me to dig a hole and bury the money."

Looking around the estate, Horace said, "If I could remember, I'd tell you, but the truth is I can't recall much of anything."

Several months later, Horace passed away quietly in his sleep.

* * *

The old de Champlaigne estate was located just off the old road to the city of Frederick, Maryland, approximately forty miles west of Baltimore. In recent years, treasure hunters equipped with metal detectors have visited the property in search of the Frenchman's lost treasure, but all have come away without success.

It is probable that the coin-filled chest remains buried far enough below the surface to be out of the effective range of most commercial detectors. Experts generally agree, however, that a very sensitive, state-of-the-art detector could likely locate the gold.

Unfortunately for those who would pursue this fascinating treasure, the current owners of the estate have refused to allow searchers onto the property.

According to experts, de Champlaigne's gold coins would be worth considerably more than one million dollars today if found.

Lost British Army Payroll

Following the historic defeat of General Edward Braddock's troops at Fort Duquesne, Pennsylvania, the surviving British soldiers retreated southward toward Fort Cumberland. Six of the soldiers served as guards for the payroll that was intended for British troops, some $25,000 in gold coins packed into leather bags.

During the retreat, the British soldiers were harassed by French troops and Indians alike. The six men guarding the payroll were dispatched well ahead of the main body and told to deliver the money to the fort at all possible speed.

Constant encounters with hostile forces resulted in four of the soldiers being killed during the first day of travel. The two remaining guards decided to hide the heavy payroll and return for it sometime later. As they traveled along a Maryland road that led to Fort Cumberland, they spotted a cave and deposited the gold-filled saddlebags within. Moments afterward, the fifth guard was killed and the other wounded.

Days later, when the surviving guard led a detail of troops back along the road to locate the cave to find the money, he became disoriented and lost. The gold was never recovered.

* * *

British General Edward Braddock was the commander in chief of the entire North American force. In an effort to drive the French from the continent, Braddock led an attack on Fort Duquesne, Pennsylvania, near Pittsburgh. When

51

Braddock's army, woefully lacking in manpower, arms, and supplies, arrived at a point about eight miles from the fort, they were attacked by an advance guard of French and Indians. The panicked British soldiers retreated in a disorderly fashion and were subsequently surprised by a stronger force of French soldiers coming from another direction.

During the battle, which lasted three hours, over half the British forces were killed or wounded, with the remainder fleeing into the Pennsylvania woods. Braddock himself was severely wounded and died three days later.

Traveling with the British soldiers was a paymaster who had been given the responsibility of distributing the military wages to the soldiers. During what historians call "Braddock's Retreat," the paymaster assigned six soldiers to guard the payroll and gave them instructions to pack the gold coins onto the fastest horses they could find and hasten their way back to Fort Cumberland in western Maryland. The fleeing troops constantly suffered ambushes from French soldiers as well as Indians.

On several occasions during the next few days, the guards were forced to leave the trail and hide among trees and rocks to avoid Indians and French soldiers. More than once they were spotted, shot at, and chased. Having to make their way through unknown forest far from the main roads, the guards became lost and wandered for days in the woods many miles east of the trail to Fort Cumberland. Additional skirmishes with the enemy forced them farther and farther from the main route until they finally came upon an old military road about forty miles east of the fort in Maryland.

By the time they were a long day's ride from Fort Cumberland, the soldiers rode into yet another ambush, and two of them were killed immediately. During the next hour, two more were killed. The surviving guards loaded all the gold-filled packs onto their horses and continued on their way. The additional weight of the gold proved to be too much for the mounts. Sensing that the horses were tiring rapidly under the load, the guards decided to hide the payroll, make their way to the fort, and return for it later.

A stream paralleled the road along which the guards traveled. At a point where the water split and flowed around a large boulder, one of the men spotted a shallow cave among the rocks sloping toward the north. They rode toward it, pulled the heavy, gold-filled saddlebags from the horses, and stacked them inside the cave. After covering them with dirt, leaves, and brush, the two remounted and continued on their way.

Moments later, one of them was killed by a bullet from an Indian's musket. A second shot wounded the other, who fell from his horse and fled into the dense forest. Dazed and weak, the surviving guard wandered generally westward, living on berries and roots, until he was found ten days later by a contingent of British soldiers. After he was carried to Fort Cumberland, the guard related the details of the flight along the military road, the deaths of his companions, and the hiding of the payroll in the cave.

Several days later, when the guard was able to travel, he was assigned to lead a platoon to the cave to retrieve the payroll. When the soldiers arrived in the area where the guard believed the cave was located, he became confused. He was unable to find the large boulder in the stream or the body of the guard who was killed soon after the payroll was hidden. Although several caves were found among the rocks and searched, none of them contained the gold.

After three days of searching for the payroll and not finding it, the platoon finally returned to Fort Cumberland.

Some of the officers stationed at the fort suspected the guard hid the money and intended to keep it for himself. Others believed that, as a result of being wounded and fleeing on foot from the enemy, he simply became confused and could not remember landmarks and directions correctly.

* * *

In 1881, a hunter found a few scattered and weathered bones on the forest floor not far from the town of Piney Grove. Among the bones were some rusted buttons. The bones were later identified as human and the buttons as the kind used by British soldiers during the French and Indian War.

A few researchers familiar with the story of the lost British payroll believed the bones were the remains of one of the guards that was killed either just prior to or immediately after the gold was hidden. Several months later, when asked to lead a group of treasure hunters back to the place where the bones were found, the hunter could not remember the exact location.

* * *

In 1907, a woodsman who earned a meager living trapping for furs in the northern Maryland and southern Pennsylvania mountains took shelter in a small cave during a violent rainstorm. As he waited for the storm to abate, he scooped together a pile dry leaves and twigs to start a fire for warmth. In the process, he discovered a piece of rotted leather that appeared as if it had come from a saddlebag. More concerned with his own comfort than anything else, the trapper kindled a blaze and warmed himself by the fire until the rain stopped. Thinking no more about the piece of leather, he left the cave.

Several years later after relating the incident to a friend, the trapper was told the story of the lost British payroll. Firmly believing he had accidentally discovered the cave in which the gold-filled leather saddlebags were hidden, he made several attempts to relocate it, but he was never successful.

* * *

Following a three-day rainstorm during a cold 1941 October, a man was hiking along the old military road in Maryland's eastern Allegany County when he spotted a gleam from something lying in the road. When he investigated, he discovered a gold British coin! Casting about for others, the hiker noticed several small rivulets on the adjacent slope, thin incisions into the soft soil caused by the runoff from the rainfall. Thinking the coin might have been washed down from a higher level, he climbed a few steps onto the low slope and was rewarded by the discovery of yet another coin. A few paces later, the soil gave way to a rock outcrop. Though he searched for two hours, the hiker found no more coins.

Eight months later, the hiker learned about the lost British army payroll supposedly hidden in a cave near where he found the coins. The hiker was convinced that the runoff had somehow washed some of the loose coins from the cave, down the slope, and finally onto the road. Determined to locate the source of the gold, the hiker returned to the area. As it was June, the slope was covered in summer grasses and the region looked somewhat different. Though he searched several times during the next two months, he never found anything. The hiker returned to the area the following October after another severe rainstorm in the hope that history would repeat itself, but success was not to be had.

* * *

General Edward Braddock's lost payroll has intrigued scholars for over two centuries. While many place the location somewhere between twenty and thirty miles east of what is now Cumberland, Maryland, some maintain the payroll never made it that far, believing it was buried in Pennsylvania.

Most of the available evidence, however, points to the Maryland location, and that is where searchers have concentrated their efforts for decades.

A coin collector, on being asked to suggest the potential worth of the 1755 $25,000 coin cache, suggested that the historical value alone was almost impossible to calculate.

Senator Perry's Lost Treasure

William Perry II was a prominent Maryland politician during the last decade of the 1700s. Rising in prestige and influence during his years in the Senate, Perry managed, as a result of astute business deals and preferential treatment, to amass a sizeable fortune. Most of his wealth remained in gold and silver coins, and he occasionally converted some into precious jewelry. It was widely rumored around the Chesapeake Bay country that Perry was very fond of emeralds.

Prior to being elected to the Maryland Senate, Perry was a successful farmer and owned a large plantation in Talbot County, not far from the small Maryland town of Easton. Perry's fine house was referred to by Talbot County residents as Perry Hall, and it was often the site for grand high society balls and parties.

After dabbling in county politics for several years, Perry became convinced he was suited for bigger and better things, so he ran for and won the office of state senator.

During the time Perry lived in Talbot County, there were no banks in the area. When the legislature was not in session, Perry kept his gold, silver, and jewels hidden in a large bedroom closet. Fascinated by his wealth and impressed with his ability to obtain it, Perry spent many satisfying hours counting his money and admiring his emeralds.

William Perry was afraid to leave his fortune in the house, however, when the legislature was meeting. He was concerned the home might be robbed or burned down and that he would lose his wealth. Wealth and prestige were everything to Perry.

Like many people who either did not have access to banks or simply did not trust them, Perry decided to hide his fortune somewhere on his property. Prior to departing for the capital, Annapolis, Perry, with the help of his personal servant, would carry the metal boxes filled with gold and silver coins and jewelry to some location on the farm and bury them. When the legislative session was concluded, the senator raced back to Perry Hall, dug up his wealth, and returned it to the house.

This sequence was repeated several times over four years.

In 1799, just prior to the opening of the legislative session, Perry and the servant reburied the fortune, which by this time was considerable. No estimate was ever given, but it is believed that Perry's gold, silver, and jewels filled six metal boxes. After making certain the hiding place could not be detected, Perry and his servant traveled to Annapolis.

Three weeks after the session started, Perry suffered a severe heart attack and died three days later. After making arrangements to have Senator Perry's body delivered to Perry Hall for burial, the servant, riding back in the senator's carriage, was killed in an accident.

With the deaths of Perry and the servant, no one was left alive who knew the location of the senator's buried wealth.

* * *

It was widely known that Senator Perry hid his sizeable fortune someplace on his plantation, and at the news of his death, dozens of searchers came from miles around to try to find it. Until order was reestablished by the local constable, treasure hunters dug hundreds of holes on the property and even removed boards from the walls of the house.

By 1830, however, most people had forgotten about the senator's fortune, and few ever visited the old plantation any more.

* * *

By the 1840s, the original Perry Hall had fallen to ruin. The new owners of the property set fire to the remains and converted what was once the yard that surrounded the fine house into additional cropland.

One spring, while one of the workers was breaking up the sod of the former front lawn of the Perry house, the blade of the plow turned up a rusted metal box. Pausing to investigate, the worker examined the box and found it locked with a simple hasp. On shaking it, he could hear what he thought were stones rattling around inside.

Finding a rock nearby, the worker broke the hasp, opened the box, and found it filled with brilliant green stones. Believing the container once belonged to a child and that the stones were mere playthings, he selected one of the larger ones, placed it in his pocket, and tossed the rest out onto the ground. Leaving the box where it lay, the worker continued with his plowing.

That night, when the worker returned to his quarters, he pulled the shiny green stone from his pocket and presented it to his six-year-old daughter. Fascinated with the pretty rock, she kept it in a small cloth pouch on the table beside her bed.

Years passed; the little girl grew into a young woman and eventually was sent to school in Baltimore. Along with her clothes and other belongings, she took the green stone to remember her father, who had died two years earlier.

During her second year in school, the girl's aunt wanted to have a special Christmas party for her and her friends. The aunt, who looked after the girl, often held functions at her Baltimore home for the students of the school. For a Christmas present, the aunt had the girl's pretty stone arranged in a delicate gold setting and attached as a pendant to a beautiful gold necklace. Proud of the necklace, the girl wore it at every important event she attended during her school years.

A year after graduation, the young girl met and fell in love with John B. Russell, a physician. During their courtship, Russell remained curious about the beautiful necklace, wondering what kind of stone it was that dangled from the exquisite gold links. The girl always told him it was just a pretty rock her father had found in a field while plowing.

At his request, the girl allowed Russell to have the stone examined by a jeweler in New York City. To his astonishment and subsequently to hers, the stone was identified as an emerald of great value.

The girl then related to Russell what her father told her when he found the stone, about the metal box filled with green rocks, rocks that he thought were worthless and simply threw across the ground. When the girl told Russell her father worked on a plantation once owned by the late Senator William Perry II, the physician recalled a tale about Perry burying his wealth on his grounds and that Perry was alleged to have possessed a number of fine emeralds. After thoroughly researching the story and interviewing several old Talbot County residents, Russell came away convinced the emerald came from Perry's cache.

As soon as his schedule permitted, Russell traveled from Baltimore to Easton and made arrangements to be taken to the location of the old Perry Hall. On arriving, all he found was plowed ground; there was nothing left of the beautiful house, the barn, or any of the outbuildings. Nor was there any indication where they once set on the property. Though

Russell spent two days sifting through the dirt of the plowed field in the hope of finding emeralds and metal containers, he came away disappointed.

* * *

Researchers of tales of lost treasure in Maryland are convinced beyond any doubt that the young girl's emerald came from one of William Perry's metal boxes that he buried near his house. The researchers also are convinced that the loose emeralds the worker threw onto the ground are still there somewhere, most likely mixed in with the soil.

It also is believed that at least five other metal boxes filled with gold and silver coins are lying nearby, approximately two feet below the surface.

Maryland's Lost Silver Mine

While the state of Maryland has served as a setting for a number of exciting tales of buried treasures over the years, it has seldom been associated with lost mines. One such tale does exist, however, and it involves a silver mine that, according to Indian legend, allegedly exists in the north-central part of the state near the Pennsylvania border. The mine, say researchers, was well known among the area tribes and supposedly yielded the precious metal for many generations until it was finally covered up and hidden.

* * *

John Ahrwud owned a blacksmith shop in the tiny Maryland settlement of Silver Run in Carroll County. So skilled was Ahrwud (sometimes spelled Arwood) that settlers from neighboring communities as far as ten miles away would bring knives to be sharpened, horses to be shod, and farm implements to be repaired.

During the 1760s, many of north-central Maryland's citizens possessed little in the way of ready and available cash, and Ahrwud, a generous man, often extended credit, occasionally accepted chickens and geese as payment, and sometimes didn't even charge at all.

Ahrwud was particularly kind to the local Indians. For the most part, the Indians lived in poor dwellings back in the woods, had little to eat, and rarely had any money. After repairing a tool or sharpening an axe for one of the Indians, Ahrwud would often explain that the work was free that day.

The Indians were grateful to the friendly blacksmith and came to respect and admire him.

One day, an elderly member of a local tribe carried a small wrapped bundle into Ahrwud's shop. After removing the cloth cover, he held up a fist-sized piece of silver ore and handed it to the blacksmith. Impressed with the purity of the ore, Ahrwud asked the Indian where it came from. The old man replied it had been dug from a secret mine, one that was known only to members of the tribe, a mine that was hidden far back in the woods. Though Ahrwud tried several times to learn the location of the mysterious silver mine, the Indian remained evasive.

The Indian also told Ahrwud that, for many years, members of the tribe fashioned eating utensils and jewelry from the silver. From his robe, he produced a rather crudely fashioned three-tined fork as an example. Pushing up one of his sleeves, the Indian pointed to a wide band of engraved silver that encircled the bicep of one arm.

Unfortunately, continued the Indian, the members of the tribe who once possessed the skills to make such fine things had lived long lives and were now all dead. Pausing a moment, he asked Ahrwud if he would consider making the silver items for the tribe.

Ahrwud pondered the request for several minutes and finally answered in the affirmative. Several days later, the Indian brought several pieces of silver ore into the blacksmith shop, told Ahrwud what was needed, and departed. With great care, the talented blacksmith made three- and four-tined forks, a number of spoons of different sizes, and several arm and ankle bracelets.

When the old Indian returned several days later, he closely examined the pieces and told the blacksmith that never before in his life had he gazed upon such fine workmanship. He assured Ahrwud that the members of his tribe would be very pleased. When he departed the blacksmith shop, the Indian left another large piece of almost pure silver as payment for Ahrwud's work.

For nearly two years, Ahrwud fashioned implements and ornaments for the Indians, happily crafting the ore into fine-looking and useful items and handsome jewelry. While Ahrwud was happy to be providing his Indian friends with the things they needed, he was likewise overjoyed at receiving payment for his work in rich pieces of raw silver.

One day, the old Indian came into the blacksmith shop and asked Ahrwud if he would like to be taken to the old silver mine. Excited at the prospect, he said he would and made arrangements to leave that same afternoon.

On the way to the mine, the Indian told the blacksmith that he would be the first white man ever to gaze upon the rich silver mine of the Indians. Heretofore, explained the old man, any member of the tribe who revealed the secret location was immediately put to death, and the individual to whom the location was given was never seen again. Because of Ahrwud's kindness to the tribe, however, the elders agreed that he be shown the mine and allowed to dig some of the silver.

After several hours of hiking through rugged, hilly woods, the two men at last stood before the entrance of the silver mine, a low opening in the side of a hill. Peering into the darkness of the deep tunnel, the blacksmith noted that the shaft proceeded downward at a sharp angle and that steps had been cut into the floor. After the Indian lighted a torch, they entered the mine.

For almost forty yards, the Indian and Ahrwud negotiated the steep shaft until it finally leveled out. Another few steps brought them to the end of the tunnel. There, in the glow of the torch's flame, Ahrwud stared at a thick, shining vein of silver in the rock, silver of unimaginable purity and luster. Using only his fingernails, the blacksmith was able to dig out some of the soft metal.

Pointing to the floor, the old Indian showed Ahrwud several large pieces previously cut from the vein, pieces similar to the ones carried into the blacksmith's shop during the previous weeks.

Just before leaving the mine, the old Indian told Ahrwud that he was free to come and go any time he wanted and to take as much silver as he needed for his work. The Indian, however, cautioned the blacksmith of two important things: First, he must never fall victim to greed in removing the silver; and second, he must never tell anyone else about the existence or location of the mine.

Ahrwud agreed to the conditions, and together the two men left the mine. The Indian returned to his village, and Ahrwud walked the long distance to his home in Silver Run.

During the next two years, Ahrwud often visited the silver mine, extracted ore as it was necessary to manufacture the utensils and jewelry for the Indians, and took some small amounts for himself.

Ahrwud's wife and daughter were growing curious about his increasingly frequent trips into the woods. Because the blacksmith had moved a small forge, some tools, and other equipment into the mine, he often remained away from home for two and three days at a time. In order to satisfy the curiosity of his family, he told them of the existence of the Indian silver mine. When he finished his story, he made his wife and daughter promise to keep the knowledge secret.

Ahrwud's eighteen-year-old daughter was not satisfied with a mere description and began pestering her father to take her to the mine. At first he refused, citing the warning given by the old Indian, but after several weeks of continuous insistence, however, the blacksmith finally agreed to show her.

When Ahrwud and the girl were about a half-mile from the mine, he blindfolded her and led her by the hand the rest of the way. He removed the blindfold only after they were deep inside the shaft.

Looking about the floor of the mine, the girl saw a number of well-crafted silver eating utensils, small silver statues, and a number of bracelets, all them obviously the fine work and artistry of her father. Ahrwud showed his daughter the thick vein of silver ore in the rock at the end of the shaft and pointed to several silver ingots he had made for himself as payment for his work.

When it was time to leave, Ahrwud replaced the blindfold and led his daughter from the mine and out into the woods. When he thought it was safe to do so, he removed the blindfold, and they continued toward home.

When the two returned home that evening, the girl, despite Ahrwud's cautions, immediately told her mother everything she saw in the silver mine. Even though the blacksmith pleaded continually with the two never to repeat a single word about the mine, they spoke of it to several neighbors within the week.

Approximately ten days after Ahrwud's daughter visited the mine, the old Indian reappeared at the blacksmith shop. He told Ahrwud that the tribe was aware of his transgression and that he was no longer welcome at the mine. Furthermore, continued the Indian, the tribe would no longer trade with him. With that, the elder turned and walked away.

One week following the visit from the old Indian, John Ahrwud disappeared. Early in the morning he walked to his blacksmith shop, fixed a wagon wheel for a resident of nearby

Union Mills, and visited briefly with two friends over lunch. Sometime around mid-afternoon, a customer entered the blacksmith shop but could not find the proprietor anywhere. John Ahrwud was nowhere to be found and was never seen again. Approximately ten days after the disappearance of the blacksmith, his daughter vanished. According to her mother, one moment the girl was outside feeding the chickens, the next moment she was gone. She, like her father, was never seen again.

* * *

Among the folktales of the Indians who resided in the northern Maryland-southern Pennsylvania region during the seventeenth and eighteenth centuries, there was one concerning a mysterious lost silver mine. For centuries, the mine provided ore that was fashioned into utensils and ornaments intended for tribal use. As more and more white men moved into the area, the Indians were forced to keep the location of the mine a secret, one known only to members of the tribe. On rare occurrences, as with John Ahrwud, a white man was taken to the mine.

From time to time, according to the story, those Indians and whites who broke the trust were killed or simply disappeared. Eventually, as the Indian population decreased, the mine was closed and covered over to appear much like the rest of the hillside in which it was located.

Today, those who study the history and folklore of the Indians of the Mid-Atlantic States remain convinced that Maryland's lost silver mine actually existed. If the stories are true, the mine may contain one of the largest deposits of that precious ore ever found on the North American continent.

Though many have searched for the lost mine for years, there is no evidence that it has ever been found.

Braddock Heights Jewelry Cache

Just west of the town of Frederick, Maryland, lies Braddock Heights, once known as simply Braddock. Somewhere within the city limits of this small community lies a buried wooden chest filled with jewels believed to have belonged to a French noblewoman.

The jewels, estimated to be worth well over a million dollars, were buried on a Braddock hillside by the man who stole them. When he returned for them two years later, he suffered an injury and died without revealing the location.

* * *

On arriving at the port of Baltimore, a mysterious stranger gave his name as Levesque. When the Frenchman disembarked from the ship that had carried him across the Atlantic Ocean, he carried only a few possessions in his arms but closely watched the unloading of a heavy wooden trunk.

On the dock, the Frenchman contracted for a wagon, had the trunk loaded into the back, and transported it to a small room at a downtown Baltimore lodging house. Here the stranger remained for several months.

During his stay in the Maryland city, the Frenchman used several different aliases while conducting business. By the time he left town, no one was certain about his true identity.

Seven months after arriving in Baltimore, the Frenchman purchased a carriage and a pair of horses, placed the heavy chest into the vehicle, and left town. He was last seen by residents traveling westward on the road to Frederick.

After arriving in Frederick, the Frenchman remained for a week in a hotel, seldom leaving his room except to dine. On the morning of the eighth day following his arrival, he once again had the trunk loaded into the carriage and drove away. This time, the Frenchman did not go far. Just over two miles down the road, he came to the tiny settlement of Braddock. As he drove through the small, quiet town, he examined it closely. One particular location—a steep hill behind a tavern—seemed to attract most of his attention. After passing through Braddock, the Frenchman steered the carriage to a grove of trees, where he set up camp.

About two hours past midnight, the Frenchman drove the carriage back into town. Arriving at the tavern he spotted earlier, he paused only long enough to ascertain that it was closed. Satisfied, he steered the carriage around to the rear of the building and some distance up the hill. Finally, when the horses were unable to pull the rig any farther up the steepening incline, the Frenchman climbed out and unloaded the heavy chest.

Taking a shovel from the rear of the carriage, he proceeded to excavate a hole in the hillside into which he placed the chest. After refilling the hole, he stood on the moonlit hillside making mental note of landmarks. Finally, he threw the shovel into the carriage and returned to his camp.

The next day, the Frenchman continued westward to some unknown destination. No one ever found out who he was or where he went, and he did not return to Braddock until two years later.

* * *

The winter of 1832 was particularly cold and stormy throughout much of Maryland and Virginia. During a severe ice storm one evening, a lone traveler riding in a carriage pulled by a two-horse team was approaching the town of Braddock from the west when one of the animals slipped on the frozen road and fell, breaking a leg. The second horse panicked and tried to run, and it too slipped on the ice, jerking the carriage hard toward a steep slope on the north side of the road. The driver was thrown from the vehicle, tumbled down the incline, and landed on the rocks below. Suffering severe injuries, he was found almost two hours later and carried into town. The unconscious man was taken to Hagan's Tavern and placed in a back room, where the owner looked after him.

On the morning of the day following the accident, the injured man regained consciousness and asked about his injuries. Hagan told him a doctor was coming from Frederick but would not arrive until later in the day. Hagan informed the stranger that one of his legs was broken and had been set by a local woman. Several ribs were also broken, and there was apparently some internal bleeding.

The Frenchman coughed up blood and winced sharply at the accompanying pain. Believing he did not have long to live, he reached out, grabbed Hagan's coat sleeve, and pulled him close to the bed. As the tavern owner listened, the stranger related an amazing story.

Speaking in a French-accented broken English, he told Hagan that he had come to Braddock two years earlier and buried a wooden chest filled with beautiful jewelry somewhere on the slope behind a tavern.

The jewels, he continued, once belonged to a French duchess with whom he had an affair. As the relationship progressed, the woman grew more demanding of the Frenchman's attentions. Since the duchess was married to a powerful political figure who had a violent temper, the lover often visited the wife at considerable risk to his own life. When the Frenchman finally decided to break off the clandestine relationship, the duchess grew angry and promised to tell her husband about the affair. The Frenchman decided that very night to flee the country, but before doing so, he crept into the duchess' mansion and stole her fortune in jewels. After loading the priceless items into a wooden chest, he took a cab to the port of Le Havre and booked passage on a ship to America.

The Frenchman told Hagan that, after living in Baltimore for a few weeks, he learned that his whereabouts had been discovered by the duchess's husband. Word had reached him that the enraged duke, accompanied by a pair of assassins, was on his way to Baltimore. With that, the Frenchman loaded up the jewels and fled westward.

Encumbered by the heavy chest, travel was slow, and the Frenchman decided to cache it in a safe place and return for it later. Following that, he escaped into the wilderness of the Appalachian Mountains, where he was certain no one could ever find him. After two years, convinced that the jealous husband had returned to France with his assassins, he came out of hiding. His first objective, he said, was to retrieve the jewels, sell them, and live like a rich man in America. He was on his way to Braddock to dig up the jewels when he suffered the accident.

As Hagan listened to the tale, he grew aware that the fortune in expensive jewels was buried on the hillside behind his own establishment. He pressed the Frenchman for details about the burial site, but the injured man had difficulty speaking and finally lapsed into a coma.

In the morning when Hagan checked on the Frenchman, he found him dead. Searching through his belongings, Hagan tried to find a map or journal providing directions to the buried jewels, but there was nothing.

One morning several days later, when the weather cleared and the ice melted, Hagan climbed the hill behind his tavern to try to determine some evidence of the location of the cache. He found none.

For several days in a row, the tavern owner scaled the hillside and walked its length and breadth. No single location appeared more suitable for burying a chest full of jewels than any other. From time to time, Hagan half-heartedly dug a hole or two in the slope in the hope of finding something but had no success.

After a few weeks, Hagan gave up his search for the treasure, but the topic was raised each night in the tavern and discussed excitedly. Before long, a number of the local patrons grew obsessed with finding the treasure. Some mornings Hagan arrived at his establishment to discover dozens of fresh excavations on the hillside.

The excitement concerning the buried chest of jewels continued for just over a year and eventually faded. From time to time during the next few decades, a stranger would arrive in Braddock and inquire about the buried chest, dig a few holes, and, having failed to find anything, return from where he came.

Today no one is certain as to the actual location of Hagan's Tavern of the 1830s. If the exact hillside that was located behind the tavern could be identified, electronic sensing equipment might help locate the buried chest.

New Jersey

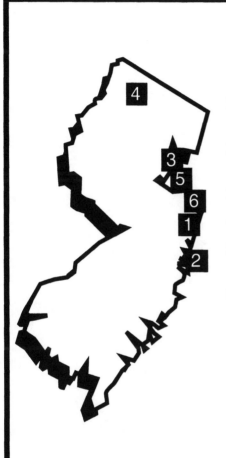

1. Jacob Fagan's Lost Loot

2. Sea Island Treasure Cache

3. Resort Treasure

4. Treasure in the Bog

5. The Lost Silver Bars in Arthur Kill

6. Secret Tunnel Treasure

Jacob Fagan's Lost Loot

New Jersey outlaw Jacob Fagan, often described as a "cut-throat" and "monster," is alleged to have accumulated tens of thousands of dollars in stolen loot during his reign as the "Pine Barrens Bandit."

Prior to Fagan's capture and subsequent execution, he buried his wealth in a series of shafts he and his henchmen dug into the sides of hills located north of Farmingdale in Monmouth County. To this day, Fagan's buried loot has never been recovered, and treasure hunters continue to comb the Pine Barrens in the hope that they might locate it.

* * *

Jacob Fagan and his gang terrorized New Jersey's Pine Barrens residents throughout most of the 1770s, leaving in their wake dozens of corpses and burned-out homes and farms. What little law enforcement there was in the region at the time was helpless against the wily Fagan and his well-armed gang of outlaws.

The ruthless Fagan was considered one of the most blood-thirsty and dangerous bandits of all the Mid-Atlantic States, and at one time the reward for his capture, dead or alive, reached five hundred dollars, an astounding sum in those days.

Fagan's gang numbered, at various times, between five and twenty. Their favored tactic was to attack remote and isolated farmhouses while the men were away fighting in the War for Independence or working in the fields. The bandits would take everything they could load onto a wagon and stuff into their saddlebags, and the stolen loot even included furniture that they would sell. After robbing a home or business, the outlaws invariably set it afire and burned it to the ground. Very few of the robbery victims were left alive, and it has been estimated that the Fagan Gang was responsible for the deaths of well over 100 citizens during their reign of terror. Over time, the bandits amassed a sizeable fortune, most of which they buried at their hideouts.

Following a robbery, the bandits retreated deep into the Pine Barrens where they knew no lawman would follow them. The outlaws' hiding places were unusual in that they consisted of several hand-dug tunnels in the sides of relatively steep hills in the Pine Barrens north of the town of Farmingdale. Once an excavation of some thirty or forty feet deep was completed, the end of it was enlarged into a room capable of accommodating at least a half-dozen men. The chamber, along with the tunnel, was shored up with logs cut from the nearby woods. A small trap door was secured over each tunnel, and when the outlaws left their hiding place, it could easily be camouflaged with limbs and leaves.

On the occasions when the outlaws retreated to these hideouts, they counted up and divided their loot by lantern light in the deep chambers while one of their members sat atop the hill keeping watch. Most of the time, the loot was buried in the floor of the dirt chamber, to be recovered at some later time.

Fagan's downfall occurred one autumn night in 1778 when he decided to rob the home of Benjamin Dennis, an officer assigned to "Light Horse" Harry Lee's cavalry detachment. While Dennis was away on a mission, Fagan learned that only three defenseless women remained at the house.

One night, while Fagan and his gang hid in the woods, a

scout rode ahead to study the layout of the Dennis farm. When the scout returned, he informed Fagan that no men were about the place and the women were preparing for bed. As quietly as possible and with only a quarter moon illuminating the countryside, Fagan, accompanied by six men on horseback and another driving a wagon, left the woods and approached the Dennis home.

Moments later, after the house was surrounded, Fagan kicked in the front door and called for the surprised women to line up in front of the fireplace. When Fagan demanded their cash and jewelry, the women refused. Enraged, Fagan decided to hang Mrs. Dennis. As the outlaws dragged the frightened woman into the yard under the nearest oak tree, one of the hired men arrived on the scene and fired a shot into the air. Unable to see their assailant in the dark and fearing they might be outnumbered, Fagan called for his gang to retreat. After releasing Mrs. Dennis, they quickly mounted their horses and fled down the road, the wagon trailing behind them.

Fagan was livid at the setback. While he was in the Dennis house, he noted many valuable items that would likely bring a good price. He assumed that money and jewelry were also in abundance in the fine home, and the outlaw was determined to take all of it. Seething with anger, Fagan began planning another attack on the residence the following week.

Suspecting the outlaws might attempt another raid on his house, Major Benjamin Dennis armed himself and several enlisted men, and they hid inside. Late on the evening of the seventh day following the first raid, Dennis spotted several horsemen and a horse-drawn wagon approaching the house.

While the man driving the wagon remained in his seat, the six horsemen dismounted and walked up onto the porch.

Once again, Fagan kicked in the door, and the outlaws stormed into the house. To their surprise, they were met with the thunder of musketfire from the armed defenders. Three of the outlaws were killed instantly. Two of the bandits ran from the house and into the safety of the woods as the wagon driver hurriedly turned the vehicle and fled down the road. Jacob Fagan lay on the plank floor bleeding heavily from several wounds.

The three dead men, along with Fagan, were loaded into a wagon and taken to the courthouse at the town of Freehold. Along the way, outlaw Fagan died from his wounds, and he and the other dead outlaws were laid out on the floor of the mortician's office.

The next night, Freehold citizens, many of whom had been victimized by Fagan and his outlaws, broke into the mortician's office, stole the body of the outlaw leader, and hung him from a tree a mile from town.

Two days later, two of the three outlaws who escaped from the Dennis home were apprehended. Both were eventually tried, found guilty, and executed.

Approximately one year later, a man was arrested for stealing a bottle of rum from a Freehold tavern. While in jail, he was recognized as Lewis Fenton, the remaining member of the Fagan Gang who had escaped from the botched raid on Dennis' home. After being informed he was to stand trial for the robbery attempt, Fenton tried to bargain with his captors by promising to lead them to what he claimed was thousands of dollars worth of buried loot in Fagan's secret tunnels located deep in the Pine Barrens. When the constable told Fenton he would not negotiate with him, the outlaw attempted to escape and was shot dead by a jailhouse guard.

With the death of Fenton went the last man who knew the

location of the Fagan Gang's secret treasure tunnels. Months later when the news of the treasure chambers was finally released, dozens of men entered the rugged Pine Barrens north of Farmingdale to search for them, but none were ever located.

In 1970, a man steeped in the history and lore of the New Jersey Pine Barrens, particularly that associated with Jacob Fagan, undertook a systematic search for the secret treasure tunnels. After examining dozens of documents and researching every scrap of evidence he could find, he armed himself with maps and set out to explore the area where Fagan is believed to have made his hideout.

Several steep hills believed to match the descriptions left behind by the Fagan Gang members were located. When they were examined for the presence of a hidden entrance, however, nothing was found.

After several more days of searching the area and finding nothing, the man returned to his home in New Brunswick. Following several additional weeks of studying notes on the Fagan lore, he decided that the hand-dug caves in the relatively soft New Jersey earth would, despite being shored up with timbers, likely have collapsed over the passage of two centuries. With that in mind, he returned to the Pine Barrens and eventually discovered the actual hills containing the buried loot.

Near the top of each hill, the searcher discovered a concave depression. The depressions, he reasoned, represented the entrances to the tunnels, entrances that had since collapsed and filled in after years of erosion and deposition.

The searcher decided to excavate one of the tunnels. After four hours of difficult labor, his shovel finally struck a solid object several feet below the surface. Moments later, he pulled free from the side of the hole a length of tree trunk that was obviously part of the shoring.

Convinced he had at last located one of Jacob Fagan's lost treasure chambers, the searcher returned home to obtain some excavation machinery and organize a team of workers. On the following day, however, he collapsed from a heart attack and died enroute to the hospital. It was believed that his efforts of the previous day led to the attack. Since the searcher made no notes on the site of Fagan's treasure chambers, no one knew their exact locations.

As far as anyone knows, Jacob Fagan's lost bandit loot is still hidden in the Pine Barrens treasure chambers where it has lain for over two centuries.

Sea Island Treasure Cache

Like Jacob Fagan, John Bacon was a well-known and feared New Jersey outlaw reputed to have hidden a large quantity of loot prior to his death. Bacon's depredations took place throughout much of the southeastern part of the state, but he cached his wealth on Sea Island, a barrier island separating Barnegat Bay from the Atlantic Ocean. Bacon's life came to an end when he was killed by lawmen, and his fortune, estimated to be about $150,000 in gold and silver coins and jewelry, remains buried somewhere on Island Beach.

* * *

The tale of Captain John Bacon, his life, and his buried treasure has been gleaned from some small amount of recorded history and a great deal of folklore.

What is known for certain is that John Bacon achieved the rank of captain while fighting with the colonists during the Revolutionary War. Even after the conflict ended, Bacon insisted on being addressed by that title. Though Captain John Bacon served with distinction and was once regarded as having a bright military career ahead of him, he subsequently resigned from the army and immediately turned his attentions to outlawry.

John Bacon was a tall, handsome, dark-haired man who carried himself ramrod straight whether afoot or on horseback. His bearing was regal and his manner precise, and in public he could be courteous and charming. Women cast longing glances at him, and men envied his good looks, poise, and confidence. Well-educated and blessed with strong leadership abilities, Bacon likely would have been a success at whatever profession he chose.

No one is entirely certain why Bacon selected a life of crime over other choices, but his first few months of pillaging made him a wealthy man, and the more money he accumulated, the more he wanted.

Before long, the southeastern New Jersey countryside was constantly terrorized by Captain John Bacon and his gang of robbers and cutthroats. Leading about fifteen or twenty hardened criminals, Bacon concentrated his efforts around Monmouth and Burlington counties and preferred to raid small and isolated farms and residences, stealing money, food, and livestock. On many occasions, Bacon and his men slew any and all who resisted them.

Because robberies by the Bacon Gang took place in remote locations, it was sometimes days before word reached area law enforcement authorities. By that time, the bandits were miles away from the scene of the crime. Bacon and his men were also well acquainted with all the roads and trails throughout the region, and they often hid in the woods and in caves unknown or inaccessible to the rest of the population.

From his outlaw activities, Captain John Bacon grew steadily wealthier as he accumulated a large percentage of the take from each robbery.

When continuous pursuit from law enforcement authorities rendered raiding and robbery difficult, Bacon and his men sometimes retreated to Island Beach, a long, thin, uninhabited barrier beach east of Ocean County. Here the gang lived in crude huts for several weeks until Bacon decided it was time to return to their illegal activities.

On a few occasions, Bacon would gather his share of the booty in saddlebags and, leaving his comrades for a few weeks, ride alone to the little settlement of Forked River in Ocean County. Here, he would rent a skiff, purchase some supplies, and row across Barnegat Bay to the privacy of Island Beach. During these retreats, Bacon would bury his share of the loot at some secret location on the barrier island, a location known only to himself. It is estimated that Bacon hid as much as $150,000 worth of gold and silver coins and jewelry.

Months passed, and the citizens of Monmouth and Burlington Counties, growing weary of the continued depredations of the Bacon Gang, demanded the capture of the outlaws. John Stewart, the constable of Arneytown, decided it was time to go after Bacon, and to this end he assembled a group of competent and fearless lawmen. In addition, he posted a reward for information leading to the arrest of Captain Bacon.

Acting on a tip, Stewart and his men eventually located Bacon at the Rose Tavern near Clamtown (now Tuckerton) in southern Ocean County. Bacon, who had sent his gang members to one of the many hideouts in the Monmouth County woods, had been drinking most of the day and was deep in his cups by the time Stewart and his men arrived.

It was just past sundown when Stewart led his men up to the tavern. Through one window of the structure, they could see Bacon sleeping in a chair, a dim lantern perched on the table before him.

After dismounting and conducting a quiet search of the immediate area to ensure Bacon's gang was nowhere about, Stewart, musket in hand, burst through the tavern door. Confronting the feared outlaw, the lawman leveled his gun at

Bacon and informed him he was under arrest.

Groggy from drinking, Bacon rose slowly from his chair, shaking his head in an attempt to clear his fogged mind. Stewart slowly advanced toward Bacon, and when he had come with a few feet, the outlaw suddenly leaped upon the lawman and seized his musket. A moment later the two were rolling across the wooden plank floor of the building, locked in combat.

After breaking Bacon's hold on him, Stewart rose quickly from the floor and backed against one wall. As Bacon struggled to his feet, one of Stewart's deputies, a man named Joel Cook, lunged forward and thrust his bayonet into Bacon's side.

Bacon, bleeding heavily, fell to the floor, but a moment later he jumped up, knocked Stewart across a table with a solid punch to the head, and fled out the door. Holding his wounded side, Bacon ran across the expanse of open ground between the front of the tavern and the nearby woods. Just before Bacon entered the relative safety of the forest, Stewart recovered and grabbed his musket, stepped onto the porch, and shot the outlaw in the back, killing him instantly.

The next day, Stewart transported Bacon's corpse to Jacobstown. While the body was being prepared for burial, one of Bacon's brothers arrived to claim it. When the body was turned over to him, the brother immediately went through the pockets. Finding nothing, he turned to Stewart and asked the lawman if anything had been taken from the body. When Stewart said no, the brother explained that John Bacon was known to have made a map of his secret treasure cache on Island Beach, a map he reputedly carried on his person.

No map was found, however, and the brother left, taking the body with him. John Bacon was buried two days later in a secret location in Burlington County.

With John Bacon gone and the threat of outlawry consid-erably reduced in southeastern New Jersey, the life of area residents and farmers gradually returned to normal. Meanwhile, word of Bacon's secret treasure cache on Island Beach spread throughout New Jersey, New York, Pennsylvania, and Delaware, and treasure hunters swarmed the narrow barrier island trying to find it. There is no record that it was ever located.

* * *

Every now and then, someone will pick up a gold or silver coin from the sands of Island Beach, now a popular New Jersey state park. In some cases, the coins have pre-Revolutionary War mint dates. Though some of them undoubtedly have washed up onto the barrier island from Atlantic shipwrecks, many people are convinced they were once part of John Bacon's hoard.

Resort Treasure

During the late 1800s, a Morris County, New Jersey, health resort was a popular retreat for dozens of moneyed urbanites from New York City, Philadelphia, and Trenton. They came to relax, enjoy the scenery, play cards, and bathe in the waters of the so-called healing springs found there.

One of the guests, a regular visitor to the resort, seldom took part in any of the scheduled activities and contented himself with solitary hikes through the nearby woods. Years later, it was discovered that the strange man was a multi-millionaire who was secretly burying portions of his immense wealth on the side of a hill near the resort. The bulk of the treasure, estimated at nearly one million dollars, has never been found.

* * *

Northern New Jersey's Schooley's Mountain was originally settled by early German immigrants during the first few decades of the nineteenth century. The newcomers found fertile land for growing crops, good graze for their livestock, and an abundant source of water. Deer and other wild game were plentiful in the woods, and nearby springs provided a continual source of fresh water. The springs also were widely regarded for their alleged healing properties.

Long before the arrival of the Germans, the Indians who frequented this region often came to the springs. Drinking the water, as well as bathing in it, was, according to the Indians and later the Germans, a popular treatment for arthritis and a variety of skin diseases. Some even claimed the magical waters cured cancer.

As the reputation of the springs spread across densely settled portions of the eastern United States, many came to Schooley's Mountain in search of cures for a variety of ailments. Gradually, more came to this pleasant countryside location for relaxation. Eventually, a fine lodge was constructed, and the area grew into a popular vacation retreat for wealthy city-dwellers.

A regular visitor to the resort over a period of several years was Arthur G. Barry. A rather reclusive individual, little is known about Barry save for the fact that he inherited an impressive fortune from his father, a business entrepreneur and shipping magnate. Barry was short, balding, and a bit overweight, and his pale skin suggested he spent very little time outdoors.

Barry always arrived at the Schooley's Mountain resort in a chauffeured limousine. Employees of the resort recalled that Barry carried far more luggage than seemed necessary, often necessitating several trips from the car to the room by two or more bellmen. According to the employees, Barry's luggage was always considerably lighter when he departed than when he arrived.

Though he was a frequent visitor to the resort, Barry never took part in recreational activities or meals with the other guests, nor did he ever bathe in the waters. He preferred instead to be alone and often was seen taking solitary hikes along the side of a low hill near the resort. It was said Barry was sometimes observed carrying a shovel with him during his walks.

Barry eschewed conversation, and when approached by a fellow lodger, he always turned and walked away. Gradually, the visitors learned to ignore him.

One year, Barry failed to show up at Schooley's Mountain, and the employees and regulars presumed he decided to visit another resort. Several years passed, and it was eventually learned that Arthur G. Barry had passed away. The information contained in his obituary identified him as one of the wealthiest men in the Mid-Atlantic States. Despite Barry's fortune, however, his bank account showed a balance of only $26,000 when he died, and relatives began wondering what happened to the money.

Some light was shed on the mystery when a New York City banker named Pierce informed the family that, on at least two dozen occasions during the six years prior to Barry's death, he withdrew large sums of money from his various bank accounts, always in cash and always in small denominations. The bills were packed into suitcases—the same suitcases Barry carried to the Schooley's Mountain resort.

From interviews with resort employees and regular patrons, investigators deduced that Barry brought his money to the resort, removed it from the suitcases, and buried it somewhere on the premises. Most were convinced that he cached all or some of it along the side of the hill on which he was often seen hiking.

A janitor who had been employed by the resort during the times Barry visited stated that the wealthy recluse would often ask for burlap bags and buckets. He told the janitor he needed them to store some personal possessions. Barry never returned the items to the janitor. On learning this, relatives concluded that Barry placed his currency in the burlap bags and buckets and then buried these objects at random locations somewhere on the hillside. Though Barry's New York residence was thoroughly searched, no notes or maps pertaining to his money or the resort were ever found.

A casual search of the hillside near the resort uncovered no evidence of excavation, but by the time the search was undertaken, at least three years had elapsed since Barry had visited the location. Any signs of digging would long since have been obliterated by time and weather.

At the request of an attorney for the Barry estate, over forty holes were dug at various locations on the hillside, but nothing was ever found.

* * *

During the mid-1880s, a series of severe storms accompanied by high winds and torrential rainfall struck northern New Jersey. Trees were blown down, the roofs of several barns were destroyed, and local creeks and rivers remained swollen with floodwaters for several days. Runoff from the heavy rains surging down a number of hillsides generated heavy erosion and some mudslides.

A few days after the storms subsided, three young boys were playing along the base of the hillside near some of the old stone structures originally built by the German settlers of generations earlier. Suddenly, one of the boys spotted an old, rotted burlap sack. When he picked it up, the aged fibers disintegrated in his hands, and something fell out of it. On examination, the youth saw that it was a wadded clump of twenty-dollar bills, still wet from the soaking it took from the recent rains. After peeling them apart, he counted fifty of them. The boys searched the area for more bills but found nothing.

Before much time had passed, word of the discovery spread around northern New Jersey, and it wasn't long before many were linking the discovery of the old twenty-dollar bills to Arthur G. Barry's buried fortune. The first persons to arrive at the location noted that portions of the hillside had been washed away as a result of the heavy storms and reasoned that some of the money-filled burlap bags and buckets had likely been uncovered and washed downhill.

Within a month following the discovery of the twenty-dollar bills, the hillside was swarming with treasure hunters. Hundreds of holes were excavated from the top of the hill to the bottom of the slope where the boys discovered the money, but nothing else was ever found.

During the 1940s, another group of youths was playing on the hillside when one of them, a ten-year-old girl named Darlene Pruitt, tripped over something. After picking herself up and examining the grass stains on her britches, she noted she had stumbled over a portion of a metal bucket protruding from the ground. The girl dug some of the dirt away from the rusted bucket, revealing a wire handle. Growing tired of digging, she tugged at the handle in an effort to remove the object from the ground. Filled with dirt and held firmly in the dense topsoil, the bucket would not budge. Repeated tugging served only to snap off the wire handle. Darlene Pruitt, carrying the old handle, resumed playing.

Later that day, when Darlene returned home, she showed the wire handle to her father and related her experience. Mr. Pruitt, familiar with the stories of Arthur G. Barry's buried treasure near Schooley's Mountain, made plans to visit the area the next day.

On the following morning, Pruitt and his daughter spent nearly two hours searching for the metal bucket on the hillside, but they were unable to locate it. No matter how hard she tried to recall exactly where she tripped over the object, Darlene could not remember. Subsequent visits by Pruitt to the area to search for the bucket were also failures.

* * *

As far as anyone knows, the greatest portion of Arthur G. Barry's fortune still lies buried along the hillside. Perhaps some future rainstorm will wash more of the topsoil from the low hill and expose more of the buckets and burlap bags filled with Barry's money.

Treasure in the Bog

Harried by the pursuit of federal troops, a group of Tories fled up the valley of Black Creek in northwestern New Jersey hoping to elude their trackers. Rather than outdistancing their pursuers, the Tories were slowed down when they encountered a marshy valley. Before they had traveled very far, their horses, already overburdened with the weight of stolen gold and silver coins, were slogging with great difficulty through the soft, boggy earth.

Fearing they soon would be overtaken because of their slow pace, the Tories decided to bury their loot on a nearby hummock. Negotiating the difficult swamp, they guided their mounts to the island, unloaded the gold and silver, and quickly buried it in the soft earth. When finished, they remounted and continued northeastward toward New York, only two-and-a-half miles distant.

The Tories were eventually overtaken and killed, leaving no one alive who knew the precise location of the buried cache.

* * *

It was a warm summer night in 1776 when seven mounted men leading packhorses galloped away from the city of Philadelphia in the moonlit night, their intention being to put as much distance between them and the inevitable pursuit that was certain to organize and come after them.

Inside the small wooden chests tied tightly to the wooden frames on the packhorses was over $10,000 worth of gold and silver coins stolen from the Philadelphia Mint only moments earlier. The coins, stuffed into canvas sacks that, in turn, were placed into the chests, rode quietly. It was the intention of the Tories to deliver the money to the British army in New York. In their wake, the robbers, all Tories, left two men dead. Intent on eventually reaching a previously specified rendezvous in New York, the Tories followed seldom-used trails that paralleled the Delaware River for several days. Near the present-day town of Belvidere, they crossed the river and rode deep into northwestern New Jersey. Though they had observed no pursuit since riding out of Philadelphia, the Tories were certain the federals were not far behind.

The country through which they now rode was decidedly different, and the southwest-northeast oriented elongated hills and U-shaped valleys bore the mark of glacial erosion of ages past. Here and there in the valleys, they skirted treacherous bogs, remnants of the long-ago glaciation.

On arriving at what is now the town of Hamburg in Sussex County, the Tories learned that the federal soldiers were scant hours behind them and closing fast. Taking time only for a quick meal of days-old hard biscuit, they remounted and guided their horses into nearby Vernon Valley. From this point, one of them calculated, the New York State border was less than ten miles away.

The deeper into the valley they rode, however, the more problems they encountered. A large glacial bog spread from one side of the valley to the other, leaving little opportunity to pass through without being forced to traverse the sticky bottoms.

Following Black Creek to a point just north of present-day Vernon, the Tories realized that the horses would not last much longer in these conditions. The mounts, burdened with riders and cargo, were tiring rapidly from negotiating the deep mud.

One of the Tories suggested they hide the gold and silver and return for it later. Spotting an elevated mound of land in the bog, they rode toward it, reaching it only with great difficulty. On arriving, they unloaded the stolen money, dragged it to a point half-way to the top of the mound, and quickly excavated a hole. After burying the loot, they remounted and continued their flight.

Just after crossing the New York border, the Tories were overtaken by a platoon of federal soldiers and, following a brief gunfight, all of them were killed. When the federals searched the men and their packs, they were surprised to discover they carried no gold or silver from the Philadelphia Mint!

Backtracking along the trail they had recently followed, the soldiers searched carefully for any indication that something might have been buried. On passing through Vernon Valley, they completely disregarded the hummock of land that rose above the marshy landscape and returned to Philadelphia empty-handed.

* * *

In 1813, two men arrived at the town of Vernon claiming they possessed information that a large cache of gold and silver coins stolen from the Philadelphia Mint in 1776 was buried on a section of high ground in the nearby marsh. The exposed land was referred to as Crabtree Island.

Crabtree Island lies a short distance north of the town of Vernon. It is an elongated spongy mass of earth and vegetation that rises some thirty feet from the relic glacial swamp that covers a significant portion of Vernon Valley.

During their first attempt to reach Crabtree Island by

horseback, the two newcomers almost lost their lives in the treacherous quicksand they encountered. Returning to Vernon, they borrowed a rowboat and laboriously paddled and poled their way through the tall marsh grasses to the island. Once out on the island, the two men consulted a map one of them extricated from a coat pocket. After surveying the island, they finally arrived at a specific location, where they commenced to dig. Following twenty minutes of digging, they unearthed a small wooden chest. Opening the chest, the two men found dozens of gold and silver coins stuffed inside some canvas sacks. All of the coins bore a 1776 mint date.

After carrying the chest down the hummock and setting it on the ground near the rowboat, the two men continued to deepen and widen the hole, but they found nothing more. Deciding to come back to the island the following day to renew the search, they returned to the rowboat. When they arrived at the location where they left the coin-filled chest, they were surprised to discover it was gone. Close examination revealed it had apparently sunk into the loose, marshy soil near the shore. Even as the two men stood and pondered the situation, they found themselves slowly sinking into the soft material, and it was only with great difficulty that they were able to extricate themselves and reach the rowboat.

The next day, the two men departed Vernon and were never seen again. It was never determined how they had come into possession of the map.

* * *

In 1863, a second attempt to find the buried coins on Crabtree Island also ended in failure. Carrying two different maps that they claimed showed the location of buried gold and silver coins on Crabtree Island, a party of seven men spent nearly one full week digging on the hummock.

One of the searchers was accidentally killed when he slipped out of a boat and sank in quicksand near the island. By the time the group departed, the hummock was honeycombed with deep holes, but no treasure was ever recovered.

* * *

For over 100 years, there have been no more formal searches of Crabtree Island. In 1990, however, a group of treasure hunters, familiar with the story of the Tory theft of the coins and the subsequent caching of the coin-filled chests, surveyed and scanned the entire island with metal detectors. They received no positive readings whatsoever.

Researchers claim the heavy wooden chests filled with gold and silver coins buried on the island have likely sunk into the soft, loosely compacted sediments of the hummock to some depth beyond the reach of metal detectors. At this writing, some effort is being spent trying to determine at what depth solid rock can be found. Some researchers contend that the heavy chests worked their way down the soft sediments clear to bedrock, and will likely be found at that level. Removing the overburden of dirt and contending with the marsh water, however, will present formidable obstacles to the retrieval of this fascinating treasure.

The Lost Silver Bars in Arthur Kill

In 1903, the ship *Harold* was carrying 7,678 silver ingots, all stacked on its foredeck. As the *Harold*, along with several other cargo ships, was towed by barges through the shallow waters of Arthur Kill between the New Jersey Coast and New York's Staten Island, a sudden movement caused the vessel to list. The shift in balance toppled the stack of ingots, which slid across the deck and plunged into the dark waters of the kill. Though most of the silver bars were recovered, a large number of them, estimated to be worth millions, remain lost in the bottom sands of the narrow passage.

* * *

During the middle of September 1903, a steamship delivered a huge load of silver ingots to an East River dock in New York. The bars were loaded weeks earlier aboard the steamer at the Mexican seaport of Tampico. The silver was mined in the interior mountains of Mexico, smelted at the site, and poured into two-foot molds. Each bar, weighing one hundred pounds, was approximately seventy-five percent silver and twenty-five percent lead. Packed onto mules and burros, the silver then was transported to Tampico, where it was placed in the cargo hold of the steamship.

At the New York dock, the silver was transferred from the larger ship onto the *Harold* for delivery to a metal refinery at Perth Amboy, New Jersey. The lighter and smaller *Harold* could more easily and effectively ply the shallow waters of the passageway. The ingots, 7,678 in all, were stacked in the manner of cordwood on the foredeck. The weight of the bars was nearly 400 tons!

After pulling away from the dock, the *Harold* was the last ship of fourteen to link up preparatory to being escorted to the docks at Perth Amboy. Around sundown, the string of ships was being pulled through Upper Bay and into Kill Van Kull between Staten Island and the city of Bayonne. By the time the convoy entered Arthur Kill, the captain of the *Harold*, Peter Moore, decided to take a nap in his stateroom. As he slept, the string slowly made its way past the towns of Elizabeth, Linden, and Carteret.

At 2:00 a.m. on September 27, as the string of ships negotiated the kill close to the New Jersey shore near the town of Sewaren, the *Harold* suddenly pitched sharply to the starboard. The stack of silver ingots, tilted at a precarious angle, slid across the smooth deck, broke through the railings, and plummeted into the waters below.

The moment the weight of the ingots was removed, the ship quickly righted itself, and Captain Moore came tumbling out of his bed to investigate the sudden disturbance. As his eyes adjusted to the darkness, he saw a few scattered ingots lying on the foredeck. Stunned, he searched for the rest of the silver bars but could not find them.

Initially, Moore deduced that, while he was sleeping, the bars were simply transferred from the *Harold* to another boat for a quicker delivery to the refinery. Satisfied with that simple rationale, Moore surprisingly went back to his room and fell asleep.

Around dawn, the lead tug *Ganoga* pushed the *Harold* up to the loading dock at Perth Amboy. As the deckhands swarmed onto the ship, they looked around for the silver bars and, finding none, asked Moore what happened to them.

Suddenly realizing something had gone seriously wrong, Moore consulted with the tugboat captain. Within an hour, the two men boarded a train to New York, where they were to somehow explain the loss of the silver ingots to distraught owners and insurance agents.

At first, Moore and the captain of the *Ganoga* suspected that the silver was hijacked during the night. When Moore related his experience of the previous night, however, all involved were convinced that the sudden shifting of the *Harold* had caused the ingots to be dumped into Arthur Kill. To the best of his recollection of the previous night's events, Moore deduced the silver lay at the bottom of the kill a short distance from Perth Amboy.

The responsibility of locating and returning the silver was given to Captain William Timmons, a veteran salvor associated with the Baxter Wrecking Company. By nightfall, Timmons, along with a crew of competent recovery workers, arrived at Arthur Kill.

Based on Moore's description of events, Timmons began his search in the mud that extended from the New Jersey shore toward the center of the channel. Conducting a bottom survey while criss-crossing the area, Timmons spent a full week without retrieving a single silver bar. Concern began to mount in response to the lack of success, and talk of a potential hijacking was renewed.

A second attempt at surveying the bottom on October 6, however, located a silver bar near Sewaren. Moments later, several more bars were found. Concentrating on this area, Timmons organized teams of divers, and during the next ten days, recovered just over six thousand ingots, which were subsequently delivered to the refinery.

On October 17, the story of the lost silver in Arthur Kill

was reported in the *New York Times*. Before the day ended, dozens of fishing boats arrived at the site, and a number of renegade attempts at retrieving some of the ingots was undertaken. Eventually, Timmons had to resort to force in order to remove the trespassers from the area. On at least two occasions, the members of Timmons' recovery team were fired upon.

By the time Timmons concluded his salvage operation and returned to New York, it was estimated that about 1,400 ingots remained lost at the bottom of the kill. Given today's value of silver, it has been estimated that the lost ingots were worth several million dollars.

When the Baxter Wrecking Company abandoned the area, a few individual attempts at retrieving the silver yielded a total of only six ingots.

* * *

In 1980, the lost silver of Arthur Kill was back in the news. Three different recovery teams announced they would try to retrieve the remaining treasure, but before a single diver entered the water, the teams began filing lawsuits against one another. At this point, insurance companies, along with some of the original owners and investors, entered the legal fray. The courts eventually determined that only one salvage company could represent the interests of the original owners and insurers. At this writing, the issue still has not been resolved, and the federal district court has not granted salvage rights.

Since the bars were lost nearly one hundred years ago, it is estimated they no longer lie atop the bottom sands and silts. Because of the relatively heavy weight of silver, it is presumed they sank to some uncalculated depth into the sediment. Furthermore, Arthur Kill has developed into one of the busier waterways in the United States. Oily residue from boat traffic and growing accumulations of silt have likely increased the amount of sediment covering the bars.

Defying legal restrictions on retrieving the silver, several small independent salvage companies have made a number of clandestine attempts at finding the treasure. None have been successful, however, and experts agree that locating the remaining 1,400 ingots will require state-of-the-art electronic bottom surveying equipment.

At an estimated value of several million dollars, the treasure may well be worth the wait.

Secret Tunnel Treasure

Near the north-facing shore of New Jersey's Port Monmouth, Mommouth County, exists a curious old home now converted into a museum. The house, likely the first one constructed by a white man in the state, is reported to be honeycombed with hidden passages, many of which have never been located. Within some of these passages, according to experts, the notorious pirate Charles Morgan secreted a fortune in gold and silver bars, gold jewelry, fine china, and emeralds.

To this day, Morgan's treasure has never been found.

* * *

Thomas Whitlock, regarded by historians as the first permanent resident of New Jersey, arrived at the north coast of what was to become Monmouth County in 1648. Whitlock, whose father once sailed with famed explorer Sir Francis Drake, was born in England and moved to New York's Long Island while a young man. Excited by the prospects of owning a business and growing wealthy, Whitlock sailed from Long Island across Lower Bay to the New Jersey shore, where he traded with the Indian residents.

In time, Whitlock grew fond of this coastal countryside and decided he wanted to live in the environs. While conducting business with the Indians, he managed to arrange time to scout and map the region while trying to determine a suitable location for a settlement. Eventually, Whitlock, along with several investors, purchased a considerable amount of land along the north coast from the natives and made plans to establish a number of farms and a small community.

Historians also believe that Thomas Whitlock constructed the first permanent house in the area. At first, a rather small, one-room log and earth structure served as shelter for himself, his wife, and his growing family. As time passed, between periods of trading with the Indians and planting crops, Whitlock enlarged the room and added a second one, built a root cellar, and fashioned a garret for storage and for his children, who eventually numbered seven.

As a result of his dedication and tenacity, Whitlock gradually built a prosperous trading and farming business. He often traveled across the bay to New York City to meet with investors and customers.

Several years after moving to the New Jersey shore, Whitlock's wife died, and following a suitable period of mourning, he married one Mary Seabrook, a widow with three children. In need of more room for his growing family, Whitlock constructed a second house only a few feet from the first. As he worked on the new house, Whitlock constructed a series of secret passageways and tunnels and added a connecting corridor between it and the old house.

As a result of increasing Indian raids in the region, Whitlock was convinced that the secret tunnels would afford some measure of protection for his family. Trap doors led to passageways beneath the floors, and some of the walls had hidden openings. It was also long rumored that Whitlock had excavated a tunnel that extended from his house to the boat dock.

Whitlock referred to his home and surrounding greens as the Whitlock-Seabrook Estate, and his plantation was named Shoal Harbor. With the success of his cotton farm, trading enterprises, and a new and thriving shipping business, Whitlock quickly gained a reputation as one of the area's most astute businessmen, and he and his wife soon became prominent in New York high society.

As Whitlock's businesses grew and prospered, he gained the notice of Captain Charles Morgan, the famous privateer and part-time pirate. Impressed with Whitlock's wealth and prestige, Morgan appointed himself protector of the businessman's shipping interests and informed the entrepreneur that, for a reasonable fee, none of his ships would ever be bothered by pirates.

Intimidated and fearful, Whitlock went along with the arrangement. Following several months of successful shipping wherein none of the entrepreneur's vessels had been attacked, Morgan demanded Whitlock give him the deed to his house and property. At first Whitlock refused, but under continuous threat he finally acquiesced. Unfortunately for Morgan, however, the transfer was not recognized by the authorities.

Enraged at this turn of events, Morgan moved onto the estate and, along with several of his crewmen, commandeered the house. For several months, the Whitlocks and Seabrooks were virtual hostages to the menacing Morgan, prisoners in their own home.

While living in the Whitlock-Seabrook House, Charles Morgan grew quite fond of one of the Seabrook daughters. When he returned from raids at sea, he often brought her expensive gifts such as ingots of gold and silver, expensive china, raw emeralds, and beautifully crafted jewelry. Morgan brought these incredible prizes into the house but soon ran out of room to store them and, unknown to Whitlock or the girl, began hiding them in the secret passageways earlier revealed to him by Whitlock.

As the booty grew, Morgan and his crewmen actually enlarged and expanded the system of secret tunnels in the houses and underground, creating an intricate network of passageways. Morgan's attentions were soon diverted elsewhere, however, and the privateer was eventually killed before he was able to return to the Whitlock-Seabrook Estate to retrieve any of his treasures. After learning of the demise of Morgan, Whitlock, unaware that the tunnels contained a fortune in pirate treasure, had them sealed off so no one could ever use them again.

Years later, David Seabrook, the oldest son of Mary, expressed a keen interest in farming, so Whitlock arranged for him to purchase some two hundred acres of prime land and helped him with the initial planting. As David's harvests eventually reaped impressive profits, he built a house for himself approximately twenty-five feet from that of his mother and stepfather. When Thomas Whitlock passed away in 1703, David connected his structure with the others via yet another passageway.

In time, David's nephew inherited the property, and during the time he lived there, he went about enlarging the oddly evolving house.

A generation later, William Wilson married into the Seabrook family. A minister, he became the first postmaster of Port Monmouth and located the post office in what was now being called the Whitlock-Seabrook-Wilson House.

During the time Wilson lived in the house, he would receive an occasional visitor inquiring about the secret tunnels and the possibility that they might hold an enormous pirate treasure. At first Wilson did not believe the tales but later became intrigued and spent considerable time and effort digging into the floors and pulling down walls. A few of the tunnels were exposed and several artifacts retrieved, but Charles Morgan's treasure eluded him.

* * *

In 1933, a stranger arrived at Port Monmouth bearing a crudely sketched blueprint of the old house. The blueprint, he claimed, was drawn by Captain Charles Morgan before he died, and it allegedly showed the locations of the secret passageways. Along one side of the map, according to the stranger, was an inventory of the immense treasure the pirate had hidden.

At the time the stranger came to Port Monmouth, the Whitlock-Seabrook-Wilson House was unoccupied, and he spent several days trying to locate someone who had the authority to grant him access. Before he was admitted to the property, however, the stranger was killed in a freak accident when he was run over by a horse-drawn wagon. The map was never found.

* * *

Today, the Whitlock-Seabrook-Wilson House serves as a museum. Hanging on the walls are numerous photographs and artifacts of a time long past. Beneath the floors and inside some of the walls, many believe a number of secret passageways contain a large pirate treasure consisting of gold, silver, emeralds, jewels, and china.

NEW YORK

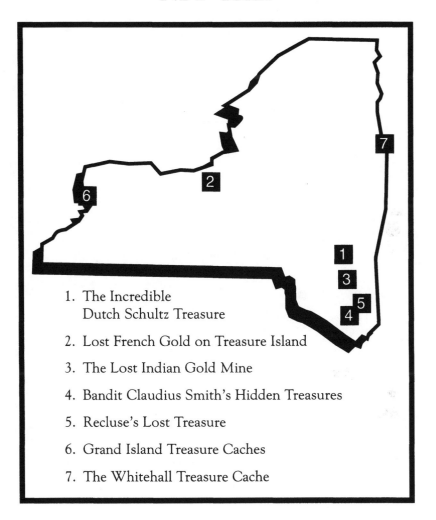

1. The Incredible
   Dutch Schultz Treasure

2. Lost French Gold on Treasure Island

3. The Lost Indian Gold Mine

4. Bandit Claudius Smith's Hidden Treasures

5. Recluse's Lost Treasure

6. Grand Island Treasure Caches

7. The Whitehall Treasure Cache

The Incredible
Dutch Schultz Treasure

On October 24, 1941, a former gangster named Bernard
"Lulu" Rosencranz lay dying in a hospital ward in New York
City. As life slowly faded from his being, Rosencranz
expressed a desire to talk to someone, and only moments
before he passed away, he related to a young nurse an amazing tale of buried treasure.

During the 1920s, Lulu Rosencranz was a small-time hood-
lum who eventually found steady work in organized crime.
Lacking the drive and intelligence to command others, Lulu
was content to run numbers, collect protection payoffs from
speakeasies and houses of prostitution, and transport bootleg
liquor throughout the Mid-Atlantic States and New England.
Some said Lulu had killed a few men, but others claimed he
wasn't capable of murder.

During this time, a mobster named Dutch Schultz, whose
real name was Arthur Flegenheimer, held a prominent position
in organized crime. By 1922, Schultz was considered a king-
pinand operated several taverns, illegal distilleries, and
assorted rackets. It was estimated that Schultz earned over
$20 million during the 1920s. As he rose to a position of power
among the nation's criminals, Schultz appointed Lulu
Rosencranz as his aide, driver, and bodyguard.

By 1932, Schultz's criminal empire was considered by
many to be the most powerful in the country, and the federal government named him Public Enemy Number One.
Though law enforcement officers tried to arrest him and

bring him to court on charges of murder, robbery, violation of prohibition laws, and numerous other crimes, Schultz always managed to evade prosecution. It was said that he spent millions in payoffs to government officials to ensure he didn't go to jail.

Though regarded as one of the country's most violent and dangerous criminals, Schultz eventually was charged with income tax evasion. On learning of his impending arrest, the gangster fled to Bridgeport, Connecticut, and gathered up $150 million of his accumulated wealth, which consisted of cash, bonds, diamonds, and gold coins. After stashing the money in a specially made iron chest, Schultz, along with Lulu Rosencranz, traveled by night in the gangster's bullet-proof Packard sedan to the small community of Phoenicia, New York, located about twenty-two miles northwest of Kingston on State Highway 28. Immediately on arriving at Phoenicia, Schultz and Rosencranz drove a short distance out of town to a bank of Esopus Creek, where the gangster buried his loot in a two-and-a-half-foot deep hole excavated by his aide.

After Schultz made Lulu take a vow of secrecy relative to the buried fortune, the two men fled in separate directions. Some time later, with the heat of the law constantly keeping Schultz in hiding and on the run, he finally surrendered to authorities in Albany, New York.

Though not wanted by the law, Lulu Rosencranz likewise remained in hiding, associating only occasionally with other criminals. One of Lulu's friends was a small-time crook named Marty Krompier, and one night, while drinking heavily, Lulu told Marty about Dutch Schultz's incredible buried treasure near Phoenicia. Encouraging his friend to reveal all he could about the location of the gangster's fortune,

Krompier eventually convinced Lulu to sketch a map show-ing the location of the cache. Once he had the map in his pos-session, Krompier began to make plans to travel to Phoenicia to unearth the treasure for himself should Schultz be con-victed and sent to prison for a long time.

Schultz did not remain in jail long because he was eventu-ally acquitted. Though never proven, it was rumored that Schultz's agents bribed key members of the jury.

Within weeks after his acquittal, Schultz moved to Newark, New Jersey, and lived in a room above the Palace Chop House and Tavern. Not long afterward, he returned to his old ways and became heavily involved in mob activity, including dozens of murders.

Thomas E. Dewey, then a special prosecutor for the inves-tigation of organized crime in New York, decided it was time to apply continuous pressure to Schultz and his gang, and he had the gangster followed and watched around the clock. In response, Schultz decided to have Dewey assassinated but made a grievous error when he went about town bragging about his plans to fellow gangsters.

Schultz's companions did not care for the idea of killing Dewey and expressed concern that, if anything were to hap-pen to the special prosecutor, the pressure applied by law enforcement agencies would only increase. Resentful of their suggestions, Schultz proceeded with his plans to kill Dewey.

During the previous few weeks, Schultz also antagonized many of his contemporaries by moving into their territories and muscling in on their activities. When high-ranking mem-bers of the mob finally learned of Schultz's determination to assassinate Dewey, they decided to have him eliminated and sent professional killers to accomplish the job as quickly as pos-sible. Within hours, the gunmen spotted Lulu Rosencranz and, aware of his connection with the mobster, shot him down. As an ambulance carried the mortally wounded Rosencranz away, the hitmen continued their search for Schultz, and in less than an hour they located him and riddled the former kingpin with bullets.

As Schultz lay dying in a Newark hospital, he was informed of Lulu's death only minutes earlier. A police stenographer, John Long, was assigned to Schultz's bedside to record any information offered about the gangster's long string of robberies. After some questioning, Schultz admitted to transporting about $150 million to a remote location outside Phoenicia and having it buried. When pressed for locational details, Schultz provided only vague directions that proved meaningless. The next morning, Schultz, only thirty-three years old, died.

Now only one man knew the location of the fabulous treasure, and with the passing of Schultz and Lulu, Marty Krompier decided to travel to Phoenicia and retrieve it. While preparing for his trip, however, Krompier discovered he had lost the map provided by the late Lulu Rosencranz. After searching through his belongings several times, he decided to proceed without it, believing he could recall the directions well enough to find the treasure.

On arriving in Phoenicia, Krompier became confused and lost, and after three days of failing to identify any landmarks as he recalled them from Lulu's descriptions, he gave up and returned home, determined to try to find the map. Shortly after arriving home, Krompier located the map and placed it in his wallet. In a day or two, he decided, he would return to Phoenicia to attempt to locate the treasure.

The next day, however, Marty Krompier was shot and killed while seated in a barber chair. Jake Shapiro, a rival gangster, spotted Krompier getting a haircut, walked into the barber shop, and shot him. Grabbing Krompier's wallet, Shapiro removed the map and fled from the crime scene.

Now in possession of the treasure map, Shapiro decided to travel to Phoenicia and dig up Schultz's treasure, but he had difficulty understanding the directions. Two days later, he was arrested in a diner in Kingston, New York. Shapiro subsequently was tried and convicted of the murder of Marty Krompier, sentenced to death, and eventually electrocuted at Sing-Sing prison. When Shapiro was arrested, he did not have the map in his possession, and it has never been found.

The location of Dutch Schultz's $150 million treasure in cash, bonds, diamonds, and gold coins remains a mystery to this day.

Lost French Gold
on Treasure Island

In 1658, a group of forty-five French colonists were fleeing New York, bound for Canada. Fearing attack by warring Iroquois Indians, they had abandoned a trading post the previous day and were making their way down the Oswego River by canoe when they stopped to rest on an island in the middle of the stream. Fearing pursuit by the Indians and dangerously burdened by the great weight of their belongings, the Frenchmen decided to lighten their load and bury everything that could slow down their escape.

Among the items buried in the sands of what is now known as Treasure Island was a brass cannon stuffed with a large quantity of gold coins. Months later, the French government decided against returning to the area to retrieve the treasure. To this day, according to researchers, the fortune in French gold coins is still buried somewhere on Treasure Island, a sandy, elongated isle lying in the middle of the Oswego River just south of the present-day town of Phoenix.

* * *

During the 1600s, the French government in Canada made plans to establish a series of forts and trading posts throughout New York. One such fort was intended for the northeastern shore of Onondaga Lake near present-day Syracuse. In 1657, Major Zachary du Puis was given the charge of leading a company of men to the region and overseeing construction of the post. After assembling a volunteer group to venture into the New York wilderness, du Puis left Quebec

on May 17, 1657. In addition to du Puis, the company consisted of forty soldiers and woodsmen, along with four Jesuit
priests. The priests intended to Christianize the local Indians
and ally them with the French cause.

Major du Puis' company was well armed—each man carried a musket along with a supply of shot and powder. A
large brass cannon that was to be installed at the fort also was
transported. Before departing, du Puis was given a large sum
of money in gold coins to be used as payment for the soldiers
as well as to establish trade in the region.

Du Puis and his company boated up the St. Lawrence
River to Lake Ontario, eventually arriving at the mouth of
the Oswego River on the southern shore. Here, the officer
learned that he would be traveling into the homeland of the
Iroquois Nation, a confederacy that included the Oneidas,
Mohawks, Senecas, and Cayugas, none of whom were particularly friendly to strangers.

After loading the supplies from the boats into lighter
canoes, the party rowed southeastward up the Oswego River.
On the third day of travel, word reached them that the
Iroquois chiefs were meeting to decide how to respond to the
intrusion of the newcomers.

On reaching the prescribed location on the northeastern
shore of Lake Onondaga, the Frenchmen hurriedly went
about the task of constructing a fortification, all the while
anticipating an attack.

Days passed and no threat materialized, although Indians
sometimes were observed watching the activities of the newcomers from a distance. When the outer palisade had finally
been completed, the workmen began constructing living quarters, storage buildings, and a chapel. When they finished, the
tiny settlement was named Mission de Ste. Marie de Gannenta.

Weeks passed with no hostile encounter, and du Puis was beginning to believe the presence of the French in the area was accepted by the Indians. The Jesuits now ventured from the garrison and made contact with some of the tribes living in the region, all of whom proved to be friendly. The priests were gratified with their reception among the Indians, and in time as many as two hundred were converted. Soon, the Jesuits were traveling deeper into the countryside to remote villages, where they held services and performed weddings and baptisms.

In October, as the first snows began to fall, du Puis learned from some of the friendly Indians that the Iroquois leaders continued to resent the presence of the French in the area. Emissaries were going from village to village issuing a call to arms, rallying the tribes to attack and kill all the French. As winter set in, however, the Iroquois decided to allow the new-comers to remain in the settlement until the first thaw, at which time the Indians intended to gather their forces to launch a raid to destroy the fort and its occupants once and for all.

Worried, du Puis began making plans to abandon the fort immediately, but one of his soldiers informed him that all the canoes had been destroyed. Believing that to flee on foot across the dangerous and Indian-filled terrain of this part of New York was foolish, du Puis devised a plan. Each night around midnight throughout most of the winter, several men would quietly slip from the fort into the woods, where they would secure tree limbs and birch bark. With these materials, the soldiers fashioned a number of primitive yet sturdy canoes to effect their escape. Two of the canoes were quite large and capable of carrying a dozen men along with several hundred pounds of gear, and the others were built along the lines of the long Iroquois canoes.

By the time the winter was drawing to a close, the Frenchmen had constructed a total of ten canoes, enough, by their reckoning, to transport them along with supplies down the Oswego River to Lake Ontario. Now all they had to do was somehow carry the boats and equipment from the fort to the river without being seen by the Indians.

Two of the Jesuit priests devised a plan. A messenger was sent to the Iroquois leaders inviting them and their followers to a great feast and parley just outside the fort. Several deer and elk had been killed and would be prepared. In addition, there was a promise of wine from the cellars of the fort. The chiefs agreed to the attend the feast, and during the third week of March 1658, nearly two hundred Indians arrived late one afternoon at the trading post.

Cooking pits had been dug and meat was roasting as the Frenchmen performed music and served wine. Eventually, the Indians joined in on drums, and soon all were dancing. Food and drink were plentiful, and after about six hours of festivities, the Indians grew weary and sought out their bedrolls.

While the Iroquois slept peacefully behind the fort, the Frenchmen were busy carrying and dragging the boats out the front gate to the shore of the lake. The gold coins were stuffed into the brass cannon, which was placed into one of the large canoes. After nearly two hours of hurried loading, all the residents of the garrison finally pushed off and paddled furiously across Onondaga Lake to the northwestern end, arriving at the Oswego River.

Fearful that the Indians might awake at any moment and pursue, the Frenchmen paddled all that night and most of the following day. Around mid-afternoon, du Puis gestured toward an island in the middle of the river, and moments later all of the canoes landed on the shore. Here, du Puis told his charges, they would prepare a meal and rest for a short time.

As du Puis stationed guards around the island, a soldier informed him that one of the boats was riding dangerously low in the water. On investigation, du Puis discovered it was the boat transporting the brass cannon filled with gold coins. Concerned that the extra weight would slow down their escape, du Puis ordered the cannon and the money unloaded from the boat and buried immediately. Several more excavations likewise were made, and other items of equipment and supplies were hastily thrown into them and covered. Two hours later, with their load considerably lightened, the Frenchmen continued downstream.

Their journey to Lake Ontario was uneventful. After remaining for a short time at the French settlement near the mouth of the river, they continued on to Montreal, finally arriving many weeks later. Not a single member of the contingent was lost.

After du Puis reported on his experiences in the New York wilderness, French government officials discussed the possibility of sending another force into the region to reestablish the fort and retrieve the buried gold. Following considerable debate, however, they finally decided to abandon plans for Mission de Ste. Marie de Gannenta and concentrate on other affairs.

* * *

Historians and others who have studied the story of buried treasure on the island in the middle of the Oswego River are convinced it is still there, lying beneath two or three feet of sand. No official estimate of the value of the cache has ever been made, and references to it in the literature only mention "a large quantity" of treasure.

Today, the town of Phoenix lies along the shore of the Oswego River just slightly downstream from the island. A pleasant community with a population of around 2,500, Phoenix has been visited by a number of treasure hunters who have come convinced they will find the gold buried by the Frenchmen over three hundred years ago.

The Lost Indian Gold Mine

Since the time of Henry Hudson, the explorer who sailed up the Hudson River in 1609, stories of a lost Indian gold mine somewhere not far from the west bank of the stream have fascinated and mystified area residents.

Indians in this region often traded gold nuggets for supplies and guns, but when asked about the origin of their precious metal, they became evasive. They told the whites that the location of the mine was a tribal secret and that to show it to anyone outside the tribe meant death. For over two hundred years, settlers in the area searched up and down the Hudson River for the mine but could never find it.

One man, a recluse, apparently did find the gold mine and became wealthy, but he died without revealing the location. Years later, the mine apparently was rediscovered by two boys but lost once again when the openings were covered by a landslide.

* * *

Early settlers in New York often heard tales of a rich gold mine somewhere along the Hudson River about sixty-five miles upstream from New York City. The stories of the mine were supported by occasional trade with the Indians during which they would often exchange gold nuggets of rare purity for weapons and ammunition and other goods. Dutch businessmen sometimes encouraged the Indians to reveal the source of their gold, but they refused, explaining that to do so meant death to them as well as to the intruders.

With the passage of time and the subsequent removal of the Indians from the region, a number of forays were made into the area by settlers trying to locate the mine. Equipped with only vague directions and descriptions, each expedition ended in failure.

Around the year 1820, a man named Truman Hurd moved into a relatively remote region just west of the Hudson River about sixty-five miles upstream from New York City. Hurd, who had fought in the Revolutionary War and was in his sixties, was considered by many to be demented. Shunning the company of others, Hurd was known to associate with only one person, an Indian named Uscong who also lived nearby. Uscong, like Hurd, was elderly and generally kept to himself. On rare occasions, Hurd, accompanied by the Indian, traveled downriver by boat to New York City, where they purchased supplies. What was remarkable about these visits was that the two men always paid for their goods with gold nuggets of impressive quality.

After two or three such visits to town, word of Hurd's gold spread among the citizens, and the old recluse and the Indian often found themselves followed when they started back upriver. For the most part, the two men were adept at eluding their trackers, but on occasion they were forced to confront them or even fight them off.

Years passed, and Hurd's trips to New York grew less frequent. One day, Uscong showed up at the home of a physician and begged him to come and examine his friend, who was very ill. The doctor accompanied Uscong on a two-day journey upstream and eventually was brought to Hurd's cabin. Desperately short of breath and too weak to rise from his pallet, the old man waved a feeble greeting at the doctor. After examining the recluse, the doctor told Hurd he was dying from pneumonia and had only a short time to live. If he had any possessions he wished to distribute, the doctor told him, he should begin making out a will. Hurd, gasping for breath, informed the doctor that all his wealth was to go to Uscong, his only friend for many years.

After the doctor drew up some papers, he asked Hurd what wealth he possessed that he wished to leave to the Indian. Pointing from his pallet, the old man showed the physician a hiding place behind one wall of his cabin in which a wooden box had been stored. After removing the extremely heavy box from its hiding place and opening it, the doctor was surprised to find a fortune in gold nuggets inside.

When the physician asked Hurd how he had acquired so much gold, the old recluse told him that, years ago, his friend Uscong showed him the location of the legendary lost Indian gold mine. For years, said Hurd, he and Uscong took what gold they needed from the mine in order to purchase supplies. Much more gold remained in the mine, he said, including raw ore from a vein winding along one wall, sacks of nuggets, and stacks of ingots. It was more wealth, Hurd told the doctor, than a man could spend in a lifetime.

Several days later, Hurd died, and the physician turned the contents of the wooden box over to Uscong. Within a week, the Indian disappeared and was never seen again.

During the following weeks, Hurd's deathbed tale spread through the countryside and excited dozens of residents about the possibilities of finding the gold mine. For years, the hills and bluffs along the Hudson River were searched for the mysterious mine, but to no avail.

And then, in 1959, the mine was accidentally discovered by two boys.

One summer day, two sixteen-year-old boys were exploring

around some low mountains just west of the Hudson River. For years, they had heard the tale of the lost Indian gold mine that many believed to be near, and each dreamed of finding it someday. Carrying only a pouch of food and some candles and matches, they set out to try to locate it.

For nearly a full day, the two boys climbed up and down the steep slopes and examined every crevice they encountered, stopping only to eat lunch. When they finally noticed that it was getting close to sundown, they decided it was time to return to their homes. While making their way down one particularly steep slope, the boys noticed the clouds growing dark and a heavy rainstorm moving in their direction. Searching about for some kind of shelter from the storm, the youths located a rock outcrop, under which they crawled.

When strong gusts of wind blew the cold rain onto them, the two young adventurers crawled even deeper under the ledge in an attempt to stay dry. Near the rear wall of the narrow space, one of the boys spotted a low opening into what appeared to be a cave. Curious, he lit a candle and entered it and was soon followed by his companion.

Crawling along on their hands and knees, the two boys covered about forty yards when the passageway opened up into a wide chamber with a high ceiling. The chamber, they described later, was about the size of a two-story house.

Holding their candles high, they looked around the chamber. One of the boys noticed that one wall appeared to have been hacked on by tools, and on closer examination, he saw a seam of quartz snaking through the rock matrix. Taking a closer look at the quartz, he discovered threads of gold woven among the crystals!

Growing excited, they removed several small pieces of the ore with their penknives and placed them in their pockets.

Near the middle of the chamber, the boys found a crucible, a rickety bench, and several mining tools. At the far end of the room, they discovered the opening to yet another passageway, which they entered. Only a few feet into the shaft, the two explorers found dozens of gold ingots stacked like firewood against one wall. Next to the stacks of ingots were at least a dozen rotted leather sacks containing gold nuggets. Stuffing their pockets with some of the nuggets and one ingot apiece, the two continued along the passageway, anticipating even greater discoveries.

For what seemed like a long time, the boys alternately walked and crawled through a shaft they believed to be over a half-mile in length. Realizing they had used up most of their candles, they grew concerned and considered turning back. Moments later, they spotted a soft light in the distance and made their way toward it. Relief washed over them minutes later when they walked out of the mine and into the morning sunshine.

They had been in the mine all night!

Looking about the landscape, the two boys were startled to discover they were standing on the side of a hill overlooking the Wallkill Valley, a valley located on the side of the mountain opposite from where they entered the mine.

They had come through the mountain!

Far out into the valley, the two boys spotted smoke rising from a farmhouse, and it was toward this they hurried. After receiving a meal from the hospitable family residing there, they made their way back to their respective homes, eventually arriving in the evening. The parents' concern about the boys' disappearance quickly gave way to incredulity and excitement when the youths produced the two gold ingots and the pocketfuls of gold nuggets.

Convinced the boys had discovered the long lost Indian gold mine, their parents, along with several friends, began making plans to return to the mine and retrieve more of the gold. In a short time, they were convinced they would all be wealthy. For the next week, however, heavy rainstorms struck the area, postponing the return. Finally, just as the dark, stormy skies began clearing, the region was rocked by an earthquake. The following day the two boys led the expedition back to the mountain, but it soon became evident that the earthquake had caused a number of landslides that altered most of the topography. Though they searched for several days, they were never able to find either of the two openings to the mine.

Several who have researched the story of the lost Indian gold mine believe it was located in either Illinois Mountain or Marlboro Mountain, each located on the west side of the Hudson River across from the city of Poughkeepsie. This location coincides well with what little information was learned from the recluse Hurd and what has since been gleaned from an examination of area Indian legends. In addition, residents in the vicinity support the notion that landslides have occurred on these mountains during the rare earthquakes that strike this region.

Somewhere inside one of these mountains, there apparently exists a rich vein of gold, a pile of gold ingots, and several sacks filled with gold nuggets. The prevailing evidence suggests entrances that lead to this impressive treasure are likely covered by landslide rubble from an earthquake.

Perhaps a future earthquake may shake the region and expose the openings again.

Bandit Claudius Smith's Hidden Treasures

As the Revolutionary War raged over portions of the Mid-Atlantic States, a gang of thugs, led by the notorious Claudius Smith, terrorized southern New York's Orange County. The Smith Gang specialized in stealing livestock but were also known to rob travelers and settlers. Sometimes the robbery victims were killed.

Smith's enterprises netted him and gang members a great deal of money, and the crafty outlaw was known to have hidden most of his share in various locations around the county. Smith was finally captured and executed for his crimes before he was able to retrieve any of his hidden wealth. To this day, the location of Claudius Smith's cached gold coins and other items remains a mystery. If found, they would be worth approximately one million dollars.

* * *

Claudius Smith's parents moved from Long Island to a remote farm in Orange County during the 1750s. The region where they located was known for years as Smith's Cove and today is called Monroe, a city of some 7,000 souls lying next to the busy Interstate 84.

It was rumored that Claudius' father had been chased out of Long Island for cattle theft and other criminal activities, but those charges were never proven. His reputation, however, was that of a coarse, hard drinking ne'er-do-well, prone to gamble and carouse with thieves and cutthroats. Though he never held a job for long, the elder Smith always seemed to have plenty of money in his pockets.

Young Claudius Smith began to take after his father early, and following the move to Orange County, the youth became involved in a series of scrapes with the law that marked him as a troublemaker and thief. As trouble between the British and the colonists began to grow, Claudius Smith gradually aligned himself with the Tories, Americans in support of the British position against colonial independence. Some claim Smith fervently believed in the British ideals and supported their stand against the colonists. Others maintain that the outlaw simply found it a convenient excuse to steal from settlers.

By the 1770s, Smith, joined by his three sons, Richard, James, and William, along with several other bandits, conducted a reign of terror across Orange County that has never been equaled. Because the Smith Gang specialized in stealing cattle, they were often referred to as "cowboys." Almost nightly, cattle, as well as horses, were stolen from area farms, herded together, and driven down the Ramapo River Valley trail to a British garrison located at Suffern near the New York-New Jersey border. Here, the livestock were sold, and Smith paid off his accomplices. As was his habit, Smith hid his share of the payment in one of several locations in Orange County.

After numerous successful raids in the region by the Smith Gang over the course of a year, Orange County farms were practically depleted of cattle and horses. Finding no livestock to steal, the gang began breaking into the homes of wealthy residents and robbing travelers along the road.

A number of less affluent residents of Orange County perceived Smith as a kind of Robin Hood who stole from the rich landowners and provided money for the poor and destitute. The historical record confirms that Smith occasionally helped out some families in need, but these acts of generosity did little to offset the contention that Smith was no more than a vicious outlaw who had no compassion for his victims. Following a raid, Smith, alone, would often retreat to one or more of his hiding places to count and cache his booty. It was well known that the outlaw occasionally traveled to one or more caves in the area, where he would sometimes remain for days. More than once, he mentioned to his companions that his share of the loot was well hidden in several different caves.

Another favorite hiding place was near the Augusta Iron Works in the eastern part of Orange County. It was in this abandoned iron mill that the gang often sought refuge from pursuit. Not far from the iron works, Smith hid some of his money on a regular basis. Several members of Smith's gang are reputed to have hidden some of their loot in some of the caves in the Shawangunk Mountains.

The beginning of the end for Claudius Smith came about when he murdered the well-liked and respected Colonial Major Nathan Armstrong. So enraged were Orange County citizens that New York Governor Clinton offered a reward of $1,200 for Claudius Smith and $600 for each of his sons. During the 1770s, these sums were considered princely, and as a result, several bands of men roamed the countryside in search of Smith and his gang.

For weeks, the Smith Gang narrowly escaped capture. Constantly pursued, they had little time or opportunity to conduct raids. Finally, the pressure became so great that Smith and his gang members, frustrated at the turn of events, broke up and scattered. Three of the gang were captured within days. Claudius Smith fled at first to New York City, but on being recognized, he slipped away and traveled to Long Island.

One group of pursuers, led by a man named Henry Titus, tracked Smith to his Long Island hideout. Pretending to be looking for work, Titus hung around area taverns listening in on the conversations of local residents. Eventually he learned that Smith had moved in with a widow in Smithtown, a settlement near the center of the island.

Enlisting the help of Colonial Major John Bush and three of his soldiers, Titus led the way to the residence. After ascertaining that the outlaw Smith was inside, they broke down the door, stormed into one of the bedrooms, and captured Smith as he was sleeping. The following morning, Smith was transported back to Orange County, where he was turned over to Sheriff Isaac Nicoll.

Smith was placed in a cell along with the other members of his gang who also had been captured. The following week, all were subjected to a speedy trial and sentenced to hang in the town of Goshen.

A large crowd turned out for the hanging, and as he was walked to the scaffold, Smith was greeted by a number of friends. Two soldiers escorted the outlaw up the steps of the scaffold, and a noose was fitted around his neck. After a few words passed between Smith and onlookers, the outlaw kicked off his shoes and nodded toward the executioner. Seconds later he was dead.

With the Orange County countryside now rid of Claudius Smith and his toughs, area residents began searching for the bandits' numerous treasure caches. William Cole, a member of the Smith Gang who was sentenced to prison, told authorities that a large treasure was buried on the farm of Isaac Maybee. Days later, following directions provided by Cole, this cache was found. Cole also related that several bags of gold were hidden by Smith in three caves, but no specific directions were provided for their locations. To date, this portion of Claudius Smith's treasure has never been found.

The caves, along with the secret hiding place near the Augusta Iron Works, reputedly contain not only gold coins but also several golden artifacts taken from churches. In addition, it is believed other items—including silverware, pewter plateware, and army muskets—are buried along with the coins.

Shortly after Smith's execution, members of his family, constantly subjected to harassment, fled to Canada. About five years later, they returned to Orange County to retrieve the treasures buried by Smith. They located only one of the secret caves in which Smith cached his loot—here they found two bags of gold coins and several muskets. Though they remained in the area for weeks searching for the other hiding places, they were unable to find them and finally returned to Canada.

According to available research literature, Claudius Smith buried about $40,000 worth of gold coins. Today, the gold and other articles are estimated to be worth in excess of one million dollars.

Most researchers believe the caves where Smith hid his loot include one near Man-of-War Rock, another near the Indian Kill River, and a third near Monroe. Rockslides, cave-ins, and vandalism have modified these caves somewhat during the past two centuries, likely impeding discovery and recovery of the treasure.

In spite of that, treasure hunters still come to the region in search of Claudius Smith's hidden caches. They believe it is just a matter of time before someone finds them.

Recluse's Lost Treasure

Ashel Bell was a frugal child born to frugal parents. Throughout his life, Bell saved most of his income, hoarding it until he eventually acquired a fortune. With some of his money, he purchased hundreds of acres of farmland that, in turn, he leased.

While collecting rent from his tenants over the years, Bell lived in caves and visited town only rarely. Bell shunned human companionship, and when he encountered the occasional traveler or hunter in the woods, he would turn and flee.

When Bell was eighty years old, he died while attempting to cross the Hudson River in the winter. It is estimated that he left behind approximately $100,000 in gold coins. Researchers are convinced Bell's fortune is hidden in one or more of the many caves in the Fishkill Mountains.

* * *

Ashel Bell, born in 1817, was the only child of Ruben and Anna Bell. The parents doted on the boy to the extent that they rarely allowed him the companionship of other children his age. On the few occasions when the young and socially inexperienced Ashel found himself in the company of others, he seldom knew how to act or respond, and as a result, his peers often made fun of him.

Bell was raised on his parents' farm in the Putnam Valley near the Connecticut border. His overly protective parents provided him with a private tutor and generous allowance. From time to time the boy was allowed to work for neighboring farmers, but for the most part, the only people he saw or conversed with were his mother and father. Over the years, the parsimonious Bell acquired an impressive amount of money, all of which he converted into gold coins and kept hidden in a secret location somewhere on the farm.

By the time Bell was twenty years old, he decided there was more to life than what he was experiencing. He informed his parents he was leaving the family farm and was going to try to make a living in New York City. Despite pleadings from his parents to remain on the Putnam Valley estate, Bell packed his money, a modest fortune in gold coins, into his saddlebags and rode away.

The young and inexperienced Ashel Bell found New York City overwhelming and intimidating and did not remain long. Clearly a social misfit in the big and boisterous city, Bell grew frustrated with his lack of skills in meeting and dealing with people. After several weeks in the crowded commercial center, Bell was ready to leave.

After considering his options, Bell decided to purchase a farm for himself, a place where he could live in relative solitude. Not far from the village of Fishkill, located about forty-five miles north of New York City near the Hudson River, Bell found what he wanted. Using some of his money, he purchased one hundred acres and contracted for the construction of a cabin and a barn. After moving into his new home, the young man hired some workers and began overseeing the production of a crop.

For two years, Bell contented himself with agriculture. He was relatively happy with his lot but would occasionally travel to different towns in the region where he would attend musicals or listen to orators. Though he tried, he was never successful in mingling comfortably with others. One day, during a visit to the town of Cold Spring on the Hudson River, Bell met a young woman named Jessica Brown. Brown, impressed by Bell's land holdings and apparent wealth, flirted with the young farmer and invited him to come courting. Bell was quite responsive to the woman's attention, the first he had ever received, and he returned time and again to visit her. Four months after first meeting Brown, Bell proposed marriage. Three weeks later, the two were wed and moved to the farm near Fishkill.

It did not take Jessica Bell long to become bored with Ashel Bell and her life on the farm. The young wife craved the excitement of the city and the company of others, but Bell would rarely agree to invite neighboring farmers to his home, nor would he leave the farm to travel to New York or even to Fishkill.

Frustrated with her life of solitude and loneliness, Jessica Bell traveled often to Cold Spring to stay with her parents. During one of her visits, she met a New York businessman named Harry Phelps, fell in love with him, and a short time later divorced Bell.

Ashel Bell was devastated by the loss of his wife of only a few months. The experience convinced him he had no place in society, and he shunned human company now more than ever. With a renewed dedication, Bell plunged into his farm work, believing the distraction would soon rid him of the memories of his recent failure.

As time passed, Bell experienced healthy harvests and usually sold his crop for a good profit. With some of his money, he purchased adjoining land until he eventually owned several hundred acres in the region. Gradually tiring of farming, Bell decided to lease his land to others and retreat into the nearby mountains.

Taking only the clothes on his back and leading two pack-horses carrying his fortune in gold coins, Bell disappeared into the Fishkill Mountains, sometimes for several months at a time. At night, he slept in one of the many caves found here, and by day he hunted and trapped his food. Two or three times each year, Bell would ride into Fishkill to purchase supplies such as coffee, meal, and tinned goods. As soon as his transactions were completed, he would vanish once again into the mountains without speaking to anyone. The only other times Bell was seen was when he visited his tenants to collect rent.

As time passed, Bell grew a long beard, and his hair, which he never cut, fell well below his shoulders. His ragged, dirty clothes hung about him in tatters, and he always appeared unkempt. Fishkill residents commented that he looked much like a tramp, and few could believe that he was one of the wealthiest men in the county.

In time, Bell acquired more property, some of it in Orange County just across the Hudson River. In 1897, when Bell was eighty years old, he left his cave in the Fishkill Mountains one morning with the intention of crossing the river and collecting rent from his Orange County tenants. When he arrived at the town of Chelsea on the east bank of the Hudson, Bell saw that the river was frozen. Having crossed frozen streams many times in his life, Bell confidently stepped out onto the ice and tested it. Believing it was solid enough to support his weight, he made his way across the river toward the town of Newburgh on the other side.

Near the middle of the river, Bell fell through the ice and disappeared in the water. Two days later, his body was found washed up on the banks near Beacon, about a mile downstream.

Following Bell's death, it was learned that he had several bank accounts in Duchess and Ulster counties, but the combined amount was only around $30,000. It was believed, with good reason, that Bell possessed well over $100,000, most of it in gold coins.

The few people who encountered the recluse from time to time were convinced Bell kept his money hidden in one or more of the caves in the Fishkill Mountains. After word of Bell's death spread throughout the area, a few men traveled into the Fishkills to try to find his cache. In one cave in which Bell was known to have resided, only a single pouch of gold coins was discovered hidden under a rock.

The largest portion of Ashel Bell's fortune remains undiscovered, and if found today, it would be worth well over one million dollars.

Grand Island Treasure Caches

Situated in the middle of the Niagara River between New York and Ontario, Canada, lies Grand Island. During the last decade of the 1700s, a wealthy Frenchman named Claireaux, along with a number of servants, moved onto the island and had a fine mansion constructed.

No one knew the source of the Frenchman's wealth. Some suspected he had been a notorious pirate; others suggested he was merely a successful businessman. It was even rumored Claireaux once had held an important government position in France and fled the country with a portion of the treasury. None of the contentions, however, carried any evidence, and Claireaux himself refused to discuss such matters with the few people he came in contact with. Once every few months, however, a ship landed at the island, and several trunks and chests were unloaded. One of Claireaux's servants once told a shopkeeper in Buffalo that the chests contained gold and jewelry that came from afar and that his employer secretly buried them in various locations around the island.

After living on the island only a few years, Claireaux disappeared, a mystery that has never been solved. Prior to his disappearance, however, no ship arrived to carry away his treasure, all of which is believed to be still buried somewhere on the island.

* * *

Two hundred years ago, Grand Island, located in the middle of the Niagara River just downstream from Niagara Falls, was a wild and forested place visited only by occasional hunters and trappers. Winters here were harsh, and for much of the year, it was impossible to cross the river. The Seneca Indians, who lived in this area, generally avoided Grand Island. Even when the nearby city of Buffalo was bursting with new settlement and businesses, Grand Island remained empty save for the occasional visit by a hunting party.

Oddly and with no explanation whatsoever, a mysterious Frenchman moved onto the island during the last decade of the eighteenth century. No one knew why he selected the island as a place to settle, nor did anyone know anything about his background. Accompanied by a number of servants, the Frenchman, named Claireaux, selected sites for a home and a large pier on the northern end of the island.

Claireaux sent servants into Buffalo to hire carpenters and laborers, and eventually an impressive mansion was constructed. Merchant vessels arriving at Grand Island tied up at the pier, and crewmen unloaded deliveries.

During the construction of the mansion, the workers often witnessed the arrival of merchant ships sailing downriver from Lake Erie. These ships carried supplies and furnishings for the wealthy Claireaux, and time and again the builders watched as fine carpets, furniture, china, silverware, glassware, and other expensive items were unloaded and carried into the dwelling.

On numerous occasions, the workers watched as heavy chests were unloaded from the ships, chests containing gold and precious jewels, according to some of Claireaux's servants. After Claireaux himself opened and examined each of these chests, he had them placed on a horse-drawn cart. Alone, Claireaux drove the cart out into the thick woods where, presumably, he buried each chest. At least six such chests arrived during the construction of the mansion, and observers suggested several more were delivered during successive years.

When the carpenters completed the construction of the mansion, they were paid in gold coins minted in France, coins believed to have come from one of the chests.

Once a group of trappers who had heard stories about Claireaux's buried treasures met in a Buffalo tavern to make plans to raid Grand Island, capture the Frenchman, and steal his fortune. By night, the raiders, eight in all, crossed the eastern arm of the Niagara River in three boats and landed on the island. As they set foot on the shore, the invaders were immediately attacked by Claireaux's servants. During the ensuing melee, two of the trappers were killed. The survivors, four of whom were seriously wounded, climbed back into the boats and rowed away.

Word quickly spread of Claireaux's defense of the island, and the Frenchman was rarely bothered again by intruders.

In 1799, a group of friendly hunters rowed to Grand Island to seek an audience with Claireaux. Each year, the Frenchman permitted the men to hunt on the island and required only that they inform him first.

On arriving at Grand Island for each hunt, the men were always met by one or more of the servants who would escort them to Claireaux's mansion. On this day, however, no one was waiting for them on the shore. As the men followed the narrow trail through the woods to the mansion, they began to get a feeling something was wrong. On reaching the place where the trail opened onto the grounds, the hunters found only the charred remains of the great mansion. Here and there, furnishings, many of which were destroyed by fire, were strewn across the grounds.

The hunters did not know what to make of the situation. No one living along the nearby New York shore reported seeing flames or hearing any commotion whatsoever. While examining the ruins of the home, the hunters found the bodies of two servants. One of them had been shot in the head. The group of hunters thoroughly searched the entire island over the next few days but found no sign of Claireaux or any of the other servants. Had the Frenchman been killed? Had his treasure been recovered? There appeared to be no answers to the questions.

The few shopkeepers in Buffalo who regularly conducted business with Claireaux maintained that several of his servants had purchased the normal amount of supplies only two days prior to the hunters' discovery and that nothing seemed amiss. Furthermore, no ships had been seen sailing to or from the island in weeks.

While no one is certain what happened to Claireaux, most are convinced that his great treasures are still buried somewhere on the island. Given the descriptions of Claireaux's treasure by his servants and the carpenters who built the mansion, it must have been worth millions, even in late-1700s' values. If found today, the treasure would indeed carry an impressive value.

Today Grand Island is bisected by Interstate 190 and is visited by thousands of tourists each year. Some who have researched Claireaux and his treasure maintain that most, if not all, of the Frenchman's fortune is still buried somewhere on the island. Unfortunately, it has been conceded that the construction of the interstate and other structures likely covered the hiding places.

The Whitehall Treasure Cache

The present-day eastern New York town of Whitehall lies near a large treasure cache that was hidden during the American Revolution. At the time, an area merchant and British sympathizer named Robert Gordon concealed approximately $75,000 in gold prior to fleeing to Canada. Killed several years later during a hunting trip, Gordon never returned to the Whitehall area to retrieve his fortune.

* * *

Whitehall is located near the New York-Vermont border near Mellawee, Poultney, and Wood Creeks. Around 1770, a man named Robert Gordon arrived in this area and established a successful trading post on the west bank of Wood Creek. Providing knives, tools, and other goods to the area Indians in exchange for furs, Gordon prospered and eventually grew quite wealthy by early New York standards. During this time, the area around the trading post was referred to simply as Gordon's Land.

When Robert Gordon sold his furs to the buyer from New York City, he always insisted payment be made in gold, and over the years, the merchant accumulated an impressive amount of it.

Gordon's trading post was housed in a large red barn. The floor of the building was given over to the business of the trading post, and Gordon and his family lived above in the loft. The Red Barn, as it came to be known in the region, served as a gathering place for traders, local businessmen, and friendly

Indians. Gordon was regarded as a friend by all of them. Several years later, when the American Revolution broke out, Gordon outwardly professed allegiance to the British Crown. Along with a number of his friends, Gordon served as a scout and advisor for British troops under the command of General Burgoyne in the eastern New York region. Gordon's efforts on behalf of the British angered many of his neighbors and customers, and most of them refused to trade further at his establishment. In addition, the American loyalists intimidated the local Indians to the point that they no longer brought their furs to the Red Barn for trade. Eventually, Gordon's business suffered, and his family began receiving death threats. Fearing for his life and those of his wife and daughter, the tradesman began making preparations to flee to Canada.

Pulling an old oak chest from storage, Gordon counted his gold, placed it into the wooden container, and secured it with a metal hasp. After loading the wagon with family belongings, the merchant was chagrined to discover there was no room for the heavy chest. Realizing that the great weight of the chest would likely impede efficient flight, Gordon decided to hide it nearby and return for it later.

Leaving his wife and daughter at the trading post, Gordon transported the chest to a marshy area near the mouth of Poultney Creek, a place known locally as the Harbor. Hiding it deep in the marsh, Gordon determined to return for it when the military hostilities subsided. After concealing the chest, Gordon gathered his family and departed during the night for Quebec. Left behind in the Poultney River marsh was an estimated $75,000 worth of gold coins. Gordon drew no map showing the location of the treasure cache, nor did he provide directions for his wife and daughter.

Shortly after arriving in Quebec, Gordon started another trading post, one that soon became very successful. Life for the merchant and his family was good in the province, and, as in New York, Gordon prospered. Though he was extremely happy in Canada, Robert Gordon constantly thought about the $75,000 in gold hidden in a New York marsh and anticipated the day he would be able to return for it.

It was not to be. One afternoon during an elk hunting expedition in the woods near the town of St. Jerome, Robert Gordon was accidentally shot and killed. With his death went the knowledge of the location of the secret treasure cache. Prior to his death, however, Gordon told the story of his buried treasure cache near Poultney Creek to a close friend.

A few months later, the Red Barn trading post was burned to the ground, and the area once owned by Gordon was renamed Whitehall by the victorious patriots.

Time passed, and eventually more and more settlers moved into the region. Whitehall evolved into a growing and thriving community. Large portions of the marsh were eventually drained and homes constructed on the reclaimed land.

Many familiar with the tale of Robert Gordon's lost treasure cache are convinced that houses lie above the area where the chest filled with gold coins was hidden, but others are not so certain.

In 1934, a work crew that had been hired to dredge the swamp and the adjacent river bed discovered a heavy oaken chest lying in the shallow waters. The chest was secured with a stout metal hasp. With great difficulty, the chest was pulled from the marsh and loaded into a rowboat. As the workers rowed the small craft toward the nearest bank, however, the boat capsized, and the chest sank to the bottom of the river.

Though several hours were spent trying to locate the chest, it was never found.

Experts believe the chest found by the workers was most likely the one originally hidden by Gordon, and that locked safely inside it was a fortune in gold coins. The chest lies today buried somewhere in the muck of Poultney Creek, its contents estimated to be worth almost one million dollars.

PENNSYLVANIA

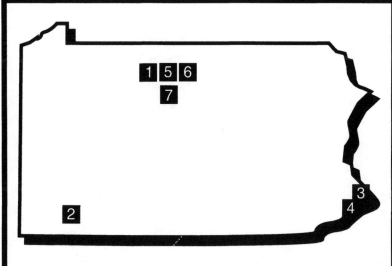

1. The Kinzua Bridge Bank Robbery Cache

2. Tons of Lost Silver Ingots

3. The Cursed Treasure of Bowman Hill

4. The Doane Gang Treasure

5. Dabold Hare's Lost Treasure of Gold Coins

6. Lost French Gold Cache in Potter County

7. Susquehanna Indian Silver Mine

The Kinzua Bridge
Bank Robbery Cache

In 1902, a young man pulled a daring robbery at the bank in Emporium, Pennsylvania, fleeing with $60,000 in cash and coins. Jumping into a horse-drawn wagon, he drove away toward the northwest and made a clean getaway from the area before any pursuit could be organized.

Several days later, learning that lawmen were nearby and close to apprehending him, the bank robber stopped his wagon at the south end of the Kinzua Bridge near the town of Kushequa. Here, he buried the robbery loot, crossed the bridge, and continued his flight toward New York with plans to enter Canada.

A short time afterward, the bank robber was captured and jailed. While in jail, he became ill and was transferred to a hospital. Shortly after confessing his crime to a nurse, along with providing brief details relative to the location of the buried loot, the robber died.

To this day, the robber's cache has never been found, and many believe it still lies buried next to the Kinzua Bridge.

* * *

In 1902, downtown Emporium consisted of a single main street along which most of the town's businesses were located. Near one end of the street, the small bank was housed in a single-story brick building. Shortly after unlocking the front door of the bank one morning, president Rupert Lyle was handing some paperwork to David Mason, the only teller, when a young man walked in. Approaching Lyle and

Mason, the man, described as being about "twenty-five years of age and of clean, intelligent features but wearing clothes old and worn," pulled out a gun and told them he intended to rob the bank. After handing Lyle and Mason two burlap sacks and ordering the two frightened men to fill them with currency and coins, the robber nervously watched the front door.

Several minutes later, the robber commanded the two men to lie down behind the teller's counter and not move for at least ten minutes. Hoisting the money-filled sacks over his shoulder, the robber ran from the bank to a nearby wagon. After tossing the sacks behind the seat, he climbed aboard and whipped the single horse into a gallop out of town along the Emporium-Smethport road. Few people were on the streets of the small town at this time of morning, and the outlaw rode away with hardly anyone noticing.

Ten minutes later, president Lyle ran from the bank to the nearby office of the constable and reported the robbery of $60,000 in currency and coins. A large percentage of the coins, according to Lyle, were gold. Several hours later, a posse was formed and set out in pursuit of the robber. With such a significant head start, however, the young outlaw was safely well along the road to Smethport.

Safe, at least, for the time being.

Before the day was over, other law enforcement agencies in the area were alerted, and in a short time the northwestern part of Pennsylvania was thick with policemen stopping and questioning travelers.

Three days following the bank robbery, a tired-looking young man driving a horse-drawn wagon pulled up to a group of men working on an oil well just south of the town Mt. Jewett in McKean County. The driver called out to the men and asked directions to the closest river crossing, and the workers directed him to the Kinzua Bridge about two miles away. Thanking the men, the driver whipped the weary horse and disappeared down the road.

On reaching the bridge about one hour later, the driver pulled into the shade of a nearby tree to allow his horse some rest. Climbing out of the wagon, he pondered his current plight. Since leaving Emporium, he had learned that lawmen were patrolling the roads, and he was beginning to believe that his chances of reaching the New York border with the loot were not good. After feeding his horse some grass that grew nearby, the young outlaw made a decision. He would bury the money near the bridge and continue on his way. If he were stopped by the police and nothing was found in his wagon, he believed they would allow him to continue on his way. Later, he would return to the area and retrieve the loot.

The young man regarded the bridge—a 2,000-foot-long metal span across Kinzua Creek, a tributary to the Allegheny River—and decided to hide the money here. In the back of the wagon was a wooden crate containing a number of large glass jars. Into these jars, he stuffed all the bills and coins. After attaching a lid to each jar, he lifted the crate out of the back of the wagon and carried it down the steep slope at the southern end of the bridge. About halfway down the incline, next to a large boulder, the robber stopped and excavated a large hole into which he placed the crate. After filling the hole, he returned to his wagon and drove across the bridge.

As the bank robber was busy burying his fortune in currency and coins, law enforcement personnel were closing in. A group of three policemen, following the route taken by the bank robber, questioned the oil well workers who had given the outlaw directions. When a description of the bank robber was provided, they all agreed it was the young man they sent in the direction of the Kinzua Bridge only an hour earlier. Riding into Mt. Jewett, the policemen immediately alerted other officers in the area, and within two hours, the bank robber was captured near the town of Mt. Alton.

The robber was jailed and questioned but steadfastly denied his role in the crime, even after he was positively identified by Lyle and Mason. While awaiting trial, the prisoner became very ill from confinement in the damp jail cell and had to be transferred to a local hospital, where he was kept under guard.

One afternoon, a doctor informed the young man that he was in the advanced stages of serious respiratory disease and was not expected to live much longer. Moments later when the doctor left the room, the bank robber asked the attending nurse to sit down and keep him company. She did so, and while she visited with her patient, he admitted he had robbed the bank in Emporium.

While the nurse listened intently, the robber also explained his decision to hide the money and return for it later. He described carrying the heavy crate of money-filled jars down the precipitous slope near the south end of the Kinzua Bridge and burying it next to a large boulder. Weakly, he grasped her arm and made her promise not to tell anyone until after he was gone. She agreed.

One week later, the bank robber died. The nurse, fearing she would get in trouble for not relating the young man's confession immediately, kept the information to herself for several months. Eventually, she sought an audience with the local chief of police and related the dying prisoner's story.

It was several more weeks before the police chief could mobilize a team to go in search of the buried bank robbery loot. Finally arriving at the south end of the Kinzua Bridge, several lawmen climbed up and down the slope in search of some sign of an excavation.

Recent rains and accompanying mudslides had apparently changed the contours of the slope since the loot was cached here, and the searchers could find no evidence of an excavation whatsoever. After a full day of searching and finding nothing, the hunt was called off.

Subsequent police-directed searches of the slope near the Kinzua Bridge failed to unearth the bank robbery loot, and eventually the project was abandoned. In time, however, the story of the buried bank robbery money began spreading throughout the Allegheny region, and many area residents, hopeful of recovering the lost cache, came to the Kinzua Bridge to look for it. Dozens of holes were dug and a number of rocks overturned, but nothing was ever found.

Today, the location of the Emporium bank robbery take remains one of the most perplexing mysteries in northern Pennsylvania. Few have any reason to doubt the deathbed confession of the young bank robber, yet the money has never been found.

Tons of Lost Silver Ingots

Sometime during the War Between the States, a train bearing several tons of silver bars bound for the Confederate cause was stopped and robbed in western New York state. The silver, composed of hundreds, perhaps thousands, of ten-inch-long ingots, was subsequently loaded onto several stout wagons and transported into adjacent Pennsylvania, where it was hidden in a cave.

According to research, this incredible treasure has been found on at least two occasions and at one time was moved from its original hiding place to another. The current location is believed to be an abandoned underground coal mine that has long since collapsed. Efforts to find the treasure during the 1960s failed, but most who have researched this fascinating tale continue to believe it exists, buried under hundreds of tons of cave-in debris.

* * *

At least eighteen men waited in the dark woods as the train approached. A full moon illuminated the railroad tracks, and each of the watchers had his gaze fixed on the boulder that had been moved onto the tracks, a huge rock intended to force the locomotive to stop. Failing that, the train would surely be derailed.

Too late, the engineer spotted the boulder and applied the brakes. Though the speed of the train was diminished considerably, the engine still slammed into the obstruction with such force that it was knocked from the track. As one, the group of men hidden in the woods pulled scarves over their faces and advanced swiftly toward the wrecked train, pistols and rifles at the ready. Stunned railroad employees were quickly placed under guard. Seconds later, four of the men approached one of the boxcars, smashed the door, and climbed inside. Here they found an incredible shipment of silver ingots. Hundreds of bars, once stacked neatly in the car, were strewn across the wooden floor from the impact of the collision. Immediately, the leader of the gang flashed a signal toward the woods, and a caravan of eighteen stout wagons, each pulled by a team of four horses, came filing out from the trees toward the boxcar. It took almost the entire night to load all the silver ingots onto the wagons, and when the job was completed, the drivers steered them across the railroad tracks and onto a road that led into Pennsylvania several miles away. By dawn, the silver-laden caravan was already twenty miles from the scene of the crime. The amount of silver stolen that night has always been disputed, and estimates range from twenty to 115 tons!

The entire series of events associated with the robbery has been shrouded in mystery. The group who stopped the train and stole the silver remains unknown. Their purpose in stealing the silver has never been clear. To what location the ingots were transported and for what purpose is also a mystery, but twenty years later, clues surfaced when a hermit purchased some goods in a Uniontown, Pennsylvania, hardware store with one of the silver bars.

* * *

During the mid-1800s, an old white-haired recluse named Dobbs lived in a crude shack near some caves southeast of Uniontown. From time to time, Dobbs would come into town seeking odd jobs, the money from which he would use to purchase food and sometimes liquor. Following this, the old man would vanish for weeks before returning.

One day, Dobbs came to town and went directly to the grocery store. After filling a burlap sack with meats, cheeses, and tinned goods, the recluse handed the proprietor a silver ingot as payment. Stunned, the grocer asked Dobbs how he came by such a treasure, and the old man replied that he found a cave filled with hundreds of them. Thereafter, Dobbs would come into town once each month, purchase food and other supplies, each time paying with another silver ingot. Each of the bars was stamped with the inscription "Government genuine, New York City."

On several occasions, Dobbs was followed when he returned to his shack. As long as he was certain he was being watched, he never approached the secret hiding place of his wealth.

About two years after Dobbs first showed up in Uniontown with a silver ingot, a group of four hunters arrived in the same town carrying over a dozen of the bars. Each of the bars bore the same marks as those found on the ones Dobbs spent in town. The hunters claimed they found thousands of the ingots in a cave a few miles out of town and intended to return for the rest.

The following day, the hunters rode out of town and were never seen again. It was never known if they retrieved any more of the silver bars, but two years later, four skeletons were found in the woods not far from an area called Laurel Caverns. Many believe that the recluse Dobbs encountered the hunters taking the silver from the cave and killed them.

Shortly after the skeletons were found, Dobbs arrived in Uniontown and told townsfolk that no one would ever again find his silver for he had moved the ingots to a different location.

Dobbs apparently also moved out of his shack, for on the numerous occasions he was followed on leaving town, he never returned to the squalid dwelling. Instead, he disappeared into the nearby mountains, effectively eluding his trackers.

Once, while purchasing supplies in town, Dobbs had too much to drink in one of the local taverns and told listeners he had transferred all the silver ingots from the cave where he found them to an abandoned coal mine. So remote was this mine, Dobbs claimed, that no one would ever find it.

Dobbs continued to come into Uniontown once every month for the next two years, but one month he failed to show up. In fact, Dobbs was never seen in Uniontown again, and the residents presumed the old recluse had finally succumbed to age and infirmity. Several people undertook searches for the abandoned coal mine to which the old man alluded, but it was never found.

Months later, a man believed to be Dobbs showed up in Latrobe, about thirty-five miles northeast of Uniontown. He was considerably different from the wealthy recluse of Uniontown, for this man was a tramp and lived under porches and in alleyways, constantly soliciting handouts from the town's citizens.

When Dobbs managed to acquire enough money for a few drinks, he would retire to a nearby tavern where, in his cups, he would tell stories of a time not long past when he was wealthy. But, he related sadly, he had lost his fortune in silver bars.

According to Dobbs, the abandoned coal mine to which he so laboriously transferred his ingots had collapsed, effectively burying the silver under tons of debris. Though he tried for weeks to dig through the rubble in an attempt to reach the cache, he was unable.

A year later, Dobbs was found dead in a Latrobe alley. He was penniless.

Considering the available evidence, there is no basis on which to reject Dobbs' claim that he once had access to a tremendous cache of silver ingots. After closely examining several aspects of this tale, a California-based treasure-hunting company arrived in southwestern Pennsylvania to search for the lost silver. A spokesman for the group maintained there was ample proof of the existence of the treasure, but the team was unable to locate the collapsed coal mine.

It is concluded, therefore, that somewhere in southwestern Pennsylvania lies a tremendous fortune in silver bars in an old, caved-in coal mine. Which one and where is a mystery that has perplexed searchers for one hundred years.

The Cursed Treasure
of Bowman Hill

Sometime during the final decade of the 1600s, a stranger arrived in eastern Pennsylvania, eventually settling into a log cabin on the side of a low hill about thirty miles up the Delaware River from Philadelphia. The stranger's name was Bowman, and it was rumored he carried with him several chests of treasure acquired during his days of piracy.

Somewhere on the hill near his dwelling, Bowman buried his fortune. A few years later, he passed away without having much opportunity to spend any of it.

Since Bowman's death, information relative to his fascinating past and the source of his fortune has been uncovered. In addition, at least two maps have surfaced, both of which purported to show the location of the buried treasure. Both, however, were destroyed or lost before they could be employed in the search.

A particularly intriguing aspect of the Bowman Hill treasure relates to an alleged curse. As a result of the deaths of several of those who appeared on the verge of finding the buried treasure, residents in the area soon became convinced that any who came close to the caches were doomed to die.

Bowman's treasure has never been found and apparently still lies buried somewhere on what today is called Bowman Hill.

* * *

Around 1696, Dr. John Bowman arrived in Philadelphia by ship. Bowman kept to himself during most of the voyage from England, rarely coming out of his stateroom. On the few occasions he was seen, Bowman deliberately avoided contact or conversation with anyone.

At the Philadelphia docks, Bowman carefully supervised the unloading of several wooden trunks and their subsequent delivery to a small house he leased in town. Three of Bowman's trunks were extremely heavy, necessitating the efforts of four men to lift each of them.

During his first few months in Philadelphia, Bowman was seen only rarely when he left his house to purchase necessary supplies in town. He seldom spoke to neighbors and never received visitors.

About one year after arriving in Philadelphia, Bowman moved out of the house and had his belongings, all packed in the same trunks, loaded into a stout rowboat for which he contracted. As Bowman sat among his trunks in the boat, four burly oarsmen rowed upstream on the Delaware River.

The following day, Bowman arrived on the west shore of the river near the base of a three-hundred-foot-high hill. On one side of the hill was a log cabin, and it was to this Bowman directed the unloading of his belongings. For much of the day, the four men hired by Bowman struggled with the heavy chests but eventually succeeded in moving them all into the dwelling.

The hill on which Bowman lived (now called Bowman Hill) was sufficiently removed from any significant settlement, and for months at a time, the only people the new resident would see were those traveling up and down the Delaware River. As boats approached from either direction, Bowman, carrying a musket, would stand out in front of his cabin and watch closely, concerned someone might come ashore.

Bowman Hill was partially covered in timber, and in this

peaceful and attractive setting, the newcomer lived out the rest of his life. When he died several years later, the first people to enter his cabin found only a single trunk that contained clothes. Documents found in an unlocked cabinet named a relative living in Pittsburgh who was notified immediately. When the relative, a nephew, arrived in Philadelphia several days later, the bizarre truth concerning Dr. John Bowman was finally revealed.

According to the nephew, John Bowman was in league with the notorious pirate Captain William Kidd for years. Bowman, who was a successful London physician, departed England for America sometime during the 1680s. After several days at sea, the ship on which he traveled was attacked and captured by pirate Kidd, and Bowman was taken prisoner. When Kidd learned his captive was a man of medicine, he told him such services were needed aboard the pirate ship and offered him a job. Kidd told Bowman he would be killed if he refused. If he accepted, he would be rewarded with a generous division of any and all treasure taken in raids. Feeling as though he had little choice, Bowman agreed to align himself with Captain Kidd.

For years, Dr. Bowman traveled in the service of Kidd, gradually acquiring a sizeable fortune in gold and silver coins and ingots, precious stones, and priceless jewelry. Bowman's share of the loot was stored in wooden trunks.

Eventually, Captain Kidd was captured and executed. Bowman now found himself freed of his obligation to the pirate and in possession of more money than he ever thought existed. With his trunks filled with an incredible treasure, he booked passage to America and eventually settled on Bowman Hill.

Among the documents left to Bowman's nephew was a

map that contained a crude drawing of Bowman Hill, the location of the log cabin, and several markings that suggested buried treasure. Fearing that knowledge of the existence of the treasure map would precipitate a frenzy of treasure hunting on the hill, the nephew placed it in a cabinet in his hotel room before leaving for Bowman Hill in the company of an attorney.

As he explored Bowman Hill, the nephew began formulating plans to acquire some digging tools, retrieve the treasure map, and return to the location to dig up the treasure. Following that, he would arrange to have it transported to Pittsburgh.

After arriving back in Philadelphia, the nephew was horrified to discover the hotel in which he was staying had burned to the ground. All of his belongings, along with the map, had been destroyed. Though the nephew returned to Bowman Hill several times over the next few years, he was never able to locate any of the buried treasure locations and finally gave up. On several occasions, the nephew was heard to comment that he believed his uncle's treasure was cursed and would never be found.

Years later, a stranger arrived in the area seeking directions to Bowman Hill. When asked why he wanted to go there, the newcomer explained that he possessed a map showing at least three locations where significant treasure was buried. He showed the map to several people, all of whom agreed it had been drawn by Bowman. Several of the residents offered to accompany the newcomer to the hill and help him dig for the treasure, but they were refused.

The following day, as the stranger rowed up the river toward Bowman Hill, his boat capsized and he drowned. The map was lost forever, and the locals quickly revived talk of a curse on the treasure.

Eventually, word of Bowman's buried treasure caches spread throughout the area, and soon Bowman Hill was alive with men digging holes at every likely site. In spite of the large number of searchers, nothing was ever found, but two of the treasure hunters died, apparently from heart attacks. According to many, the curse had struck again.

Today, Bowman Hill is part of Pennsylvania's Washington Crossing State Park, and one side of the hill is the setting for a wildflower preserve. Near the easternmost crest of the hill that overlooks the Delaware River is a tower commemorating George Washington's famous crossing on Christmas night, 1776. Not far from the tower is an oak tree that grew out of Dr. John Bowman's grave.

Not far away, according to researchers, are buried at least three wooden chests filled with pirate treasure estimated to be worth millions.

While interest in Dr. John Bowman's buried treasure is still high in Pennsylvania, few ever come to the hill to search for it any longer. Though most agree that it is against the law to excavate for buried treasure in a state park, they quietly maintain they also possess concerns about the curse.

The Doane Gang Treasure

The Old West had the James Gang, the Dalton Gang, and the Hole in the Wall Gang, all of which were associated with bank and train robberies and buried loot. The eastern United States also had its outlaw gangs, and among the most notorious were Pennsylvania's feared Doane Gang. The Doanes terrorized most of southeastern Pennsylvania, and, like their western counterparts, buried a significant portion of their robbery loot, much of which was never recovered.

Before the members of the Doane Gang could retrieve the majority of their cached wealth, they were either captured and imprisoned or executed, or they fled the country. Today, it is believed that approximately two million dollars' worth of loot stolen by the Doane Gang, most of it in gold coins, is still buried at a location somewhere along Tohickon Creek not far from where it enters the Delaware River.

* * *

The Doane Gang of Bucks County, Pennsylvania, were fearsome outlaws by anyone's standards. Consisting of five brothers—Aaron, Joseph, Levi, Mahlon, and Moses—and a cousin named Abraham Doane, the gang rampaged through Bucks and Montgomery counties between 1777 and 1783 and were commonly involved in horse-stealing, burglary, robbery, arson, and murder.

By day, the Doanes played the role of God-fearing, law-abiding Quakers who loudly vilified the British and strongly opposed the war with England. At night, however, they

162

roamed the countryside stealing and killing.

In spite of their vocal opposition to the British, the Doane Gang quietly cultivated a close business relationship with them. When they learned the British were paying top dollar for good horses and cattle, the Doanes began stealing their neighbors' livestock, herding them to the British garrison at Philadelphia and selling them for a nice profit. Many Bucks County residents believed the Doanes were actually spies who secretly aided the British in a number of campaigns, a contention supported by several historians.

Even though the Doanes preached resistance toward British rule, none of them ever enlisted in the Continental Army. Most of the able fighting men in the region did, however, leaving the majority of area farms unprotected.

In time, the Doanes grew careless and began bragging about their successful pillaging. Occasionally, they even flashed some of their ill-gotten fortune around the towns they frequented, boasting it was money paid to them by the British for stolen horses. Few people lifted a hand to oppose the Doanes, for their reputation for meanness was widespread. Those few who stood up to them often disappeared without a trace. The gang members were referred to as the "Mad Dog Doanes" by the frightened citizenry.

In 1778, the British moved out of Philadelphia, and the gang's market for stolen horses vanished along with them. For a time, Bucks County farmers believed they were safe from the marauding Doanes.

Believing crime paid better than honest work, the Doanes eventually returned to plundering. Now farmhouses and businesses were broken into with alarming frequency, and solitary travelers were often robbed and killed. Though everyone in Bucks County knew the Doanes were committing the nefarious acts, no one had the courage to stand up to them. Even law enforcement officials feared the gang, and when the outlaws showed up in town, magistrates often fled.

Following each robbery, the Doane Gang retreated to a secret hiding place located on Tohickon Creek about two miles from where the stream enters the Delaware River. Here, they stayed in a cave that overlooked a bend in the creek. Not far from the cave, they buried their booty, and as time passed, the cache grew to well over $100,000. From time to time, the outlaws would return to the hideout to extract some of the money for purchasing supplies, but more often than not, they added to the cache. Eventually, the gang members constructed a log cabin not far from the cave. Here they would remain for several days while planning the next crime spree.

By 1782, after five years of successful robberies throughout southeastern Pennsylvania, the Doanes were feeling invincible, often taunting lawmen and daring them to stand in their way.

Things began unraveling for the gang, however, when they stole a horse from a farmer named Shaw. Shaw decided that Bucks County residents had had enough of the Doanes and was determined to do something about the outlaws. At every opportunity, he berated law enforcement officials for being cowards and even accused them of being in league with the bandits. He spoke loudly and often to area residents about arming themselves and going in pursuit of the criminals.

Word of Shaw's activities soon got back to the Doanes. One night, they rode up to Shaw's house, broke in, and nearly beat the farmer to death. After leaving the broken and bloody Shaw lying unconscious on the floor, they ransacked his home, stole all his livestock, and burned his barn to the ground.

While the Doanes were beating Shaw, the farmer's seventeen-year-old son escaped through a window and ran for help. At every house he stopped, he encountered only fear and reluctance—everyone declined to come to his father's assistance. Finally, young Shaw rounded up several friends approximately his own age, who armed themselves and went in pursuit of the Doane Gang.

After leaving the Shaw farm, the bandits stopped at the home of another farmer named Grier, robbed him and beat him senseless. Not far from Grier's holdings was a tavern, and with their pockets filled with money and their excitement at a fever pitch, the robbers rode toward it.

On entering the tavern, Joseph Doane approached the owner, Robert Robinson, and began beating him with the butt of his musket. After throwing Robinson out a window, the outlaws spent the next two hours drinking, looting the tavern, breaking mirrors and glasses, and stuffing bottles of whiskey into their saddlebags. By now, the gang members were drunk on liquor as well as their own perceived invincibility. Deciding to conduct a raid on the town of Skippack in adjacent Montgomery County, they mounted up and rode in that direction.

Less than twenty minutes after the bandits left Robinson's Tavern, young Shaw and his posse rode up, surveyed the damage, and continued in pursuit of the Doanes. When the gang was about three miles from Skippack, they were overtaken by the trackers.

On sighting the outlaws, Shaw and his followers opened fire. For ten minutes, the two factions exchanged shots at one another until Joseph Doane was knocked from his horse by a bullet. At this, the rest of the gang turned at fled, leaving the wounded man behind. Shaw tied Doane securely to his horse and returned him to Bucks County, where he was arrested and charged. Capitalizing on Joseph Doane's capture, Bucks County law enforcement authorities posted rewards for the rest of the Doane Gang members, and soon the countryside was swarming with men eager to bring the hated criminals to justice.

While awaiting trial, Joseph Doane broke out of jail and fled into New Jersey, where he changed his name and took a job as a schoolteacher. Nearly a year later, Joseph's identity was learned, and as lawmen were closing in, he fled to Canada.

Meanwhile, the other members of the gang managed to escape capture. Though they were occasionally able to pull off a holdup, more often than not they were met with resistance. More and more, the gang passed time at the log cabin hideout on Tohickon Creek.

Knowledge of the Tohickon Creek hideout eventually reached farmer Shaw. After recovering from the severe beating inflicted at the hands of the Doane Gang, he swore revenge. With the Doanes clearly on the run from the law, it was now easier to raise a force to go in pursuit of them. Shaw eventually convinced several friends and neighbors to join him in launching an attack on the hideout.

In all, twenty armed men rode up to the Doane cabin one morning three days later. Pausing only yards from the front door, the force assumed the Doanes were still asleep inside. One of the posse members named Kennedy dismounted, walked to the front door, and kicked it in. Instantly, a hail of gunfire exploded from within the cabin, and Kennedy fell to the ground, seriously wounded.

As gang members and the posse exchanged shots, Levi and Abraham Doane climbed out a back window and escaped into the nearby woods. About a half-hour later, Moses Doane stepped out of the cabin into plain view and announced his surrender. He was immediately shot and killed. As the posse members gathered around the body, Aaron and Mahlon Doane leaped out the back window and fled.

Several weeks later, Levi and Abraham were captured and transported in irons to Philadelphia, where they were charged with murder, robbery, arson, and assault. They were tried, found guilty, and hanged within weeks.

Months later, Aaron was captured, tried, and sentenced to ten years in the Bedford Prison. After serving seven years of his sentence, he was granted a release if he agreed to leave the country forever. Shortly after leaving the prison, Aaron boarded a ship for England and never returned.

Mahlon was captured one week after Aaron was apprehended. Only days before he was to go to trial, Mahlon, along with three other prisoners, escaped. It was learned later that he had fled to Canada.

Farmer Shaw, along with his son, was celebrated by grateful citizens for their efforts to rid the area of the Doane Gang. Years later, the younger Shaw was elected magistrate of the Bucks County village of Doylestown. After Shaw had been in office for two years, he spotted a stranger climbing out of a southbound coach that had stopped in town. Thinking the man looked vaguely familiar, Shaw approached him and was stunned to discover that standing before him was the outlaw Joseph Doane!

Doane explained to Shaw that he had business to conduct in town and would be on his way as soon as it was completed. At the first opportunity, however, Doane rented a horse and rode out of town toward the old cabin on Tohickon Creek. Shaw followed the old outlaw, staying well behind him and out of sight. Shaw watched in hiding as Doane prowled about the ruins of the old dwelling. Every now and then, the old man would stop to look around and then walk away from the cabin as if searching for something. After a few moments he would pause and appear confused. After returning to the cabin, the outlaw would walk off in another direction, only to manifest more confusion. Shaw was convinced Doane was looking for the robbery loot most believed to be hidden near the cabin. After three hours of searching and finding nothing, Doane mounted his horse and returned to town.

On two other occasions, Shaw followed Doane to the cabin, and each time the outlaw came away empty-handed. Finally, he boarded a coach out of town and was never seen again.

Shaw himself returned to the old Doane cabin on a number of occasions to search for the buried loot. According to the robbery reports, it was estimated to be worth approximately $100,000 in 1790. Though he searched the area off and on for two years, Shaw could never find the cache.

Today, the site of the Doane Gang's old cabin hideout is within the boundaries of Ralph Stovers State Park. Long-time Bucks County residents are convinced that the lost Doane robbery loot is still buried somewhere nearby.

Should it be found today, the Doan Gang robbery cache, consisting mostly of gold coins, would likely be worth two million dollars or more.

Dabold Hare's Lost Treasure of Gold Coins

Not far from the tiny community of Roulette in Potter County lies a pleasant setting known by local residents as Halfway Hollow. In the year 1830, a sixty-year-old man named Dabold Hare arrived here and established a small farm.

Newcomer Hare spoke and mingled very little with the Roulette (then called Roulet) townsfolk. He was clearly not cut from the same cloth as they. An outsider, Hare was also a man in possession of a great deal of money, and he found few kindred spirits in this remote farming community. In addition, Hare's somewhat elitist attitude, along with his strange business practices, immediately set him apart from the Roulette citizenry. When conducting business in town, Hare always insisted on receiving gold coins as payment for his farm produce, and when he purchased items in town, he invariably demanded his change be made in gold.

Hare further infuriated the citizens by refusing to place his money in the Roulette bank. Instead, he stored his gold coins in metal milk cans that he buried at various locations around his farm. When Hare died in 1850, he left only vague and dated information relative to the location of his buried caches, a fortune in gold coins that many continue to search for today.

* * *

No one ever knew exactly where Dabold Hare came from. Some said he was once a successful New York businessman who tired of the pressures of commerce and sought escape from such in remote Pennsylvania. Others claimed he once owned over one hundred slaves and operated a huge plantation somewhere in the South. Still others guessed that Hare inherited his wealth from his grandfather, a prominent Pittsburgh industrialist.

Days after arriving in Roulette in 1830, Dabold Hare purchased a farm just outside of town at a location called Halfway Hollow by the residents. Here, with the help of two stout hired hands, Hare raised cattle and some crops and conducted business.

On the few occasions Dabold Hare went into town, he tended to flaunt his higher economic class. Often referring to Roulette citizens as "poor, unenlightened peasants," Hare refused to socialize with them. He also refused to deposit his money in the town bank, claiming it was little more than a "cracker box" and that he didn't trust the management to provide the proper protection for his fortune.

Instead, Hare told some few, he placed his money—all in the form of gold coins—in milk cans and buried them in secret locations on his farm.

When Hare sold the products of his farm, he invariably demanded payment in gold. Though he often made purchases himself using currency and silver, he always insisted any money given to him be in the form of gold coins.

Dabold Hare lived a relatively quiet life in Halfway Hollow for about twenty years, and during that time, it is estimated that he buried tens of thousands of dollars' worth of gold coins on his property.

At eighty years of age, Hare was showing signs of advanced senility. Years earlier, his daughter moved to Roulette to help care for the old man, but his independent spirit rebelled against being treated as helpless and incompetent. Though he got around with difficulty and only with the aid of a cane, he steadfastly refused to allow anyone to assist him in any manner.

As Hare grew older, he no longer cared for himself as he once did. He seldom bathed or cut his hair any more, and the few times he was seen in public, he looked much like a poor tramp with long white hair and unkempt beard.

Hare occasionally went for long walks in the woods or along the riverbank. Invariably, the old man became disoriented and lost during these outings, sometimes straying miles from town. One party after another would go out in search of Hare and return him to his home.

Over a period of several years, Hare's daughter attempted to get him to tell her where his gold-filled milk cans were buried. Hare always refused her requests, claiming he was not ready to reveal the secret locations of his wealth. In time, however, the daughter became convinced her father had simply forgotten where he hid them.

One morning in April 1850, Hare went for a walk along a dirt trail that paralleled the Allegheny River. Presently, he came to a plank footbridge, the only crossing for miles. Since his daughter lived on the other side of the river, Hare decided to cross over and visit her.

When Hare was approximately halfway across the bridge, the structure, weakened by recent floods, collapsed and spilled the old man into the rushing waters of the Allegheny.

It was several days before anyone noticed Hare was missing. Another search party was formed, and within hours his cane was found washed up on the north bank of the river about a mile from the bridge. Two days later, Hare's body was discovered caught among the limbs of some downed trees nearly twelve miles from the collapsed bridge.

Within a week following Dabold Hare's funeral, his daughter decided to search for the buried coin caches. After hiring three Roulette laborers, she steered them to a variety of locations on the old man's farm and had them excavate well over two dozen holes. Nothing was ever found.

Weeks later, while examining some of her late father's belongings, Hare's daughter encountered a very old and barely legible map that appeared to show the locations of the buried milk cans. Using the map, the daughter tried once again to find her father's fortune. The first of the locations at which she dug yielded nothing. The second location likewise proved fruitless. At the third, however, a metal milk can filled to the top with gold coins was found. None of the other locations indicated on the map yielded anything.

It has been estimated that Dabold Hare buried approximately one dozen such cans, each filled with gold coins. Somewhere on the old Hare farm in the hollow just outside of the town of Roulette, this long lost treasure, likely worth well over a million dollars, still lures searchers.

Lost French Gold Cache in Potter County

During the 1690s, a large shipment of gold coins, bound for the French government in Montreal, was unloaded at the New Orleans docks. A party of voyageurs to whom the gold was consigned undertook to deliver the fortune all the way from the Gulf Coast to Quebec, an incredible distance through country largely inhabited by unfriendly Indians.

While transporting the gold, the voyageurs were exposed to incredible hardship and danger. By the time they reached Pennsylvania, warring Seneca Indians caused them to alter their route. While fleeing from their pursuers, the Frenchmen hurriedly buried the gold somewhere in the Valley of Borie in Potter County.

The voyageurs never returned to retrieve the gold, and the fortune, which was transported in several small, wooden kegs, has been the subject of dozens of organized searches over nearly three centuries.

* * *

During the latter part of the seventeenth century, funds were desperately needed by the French government in Montreal. Money was in short supply in the newly settled lands, money necessary for investing in the fur trade and paying the French troops stationed in the region. The economic situation was growing serious as a result of British warships intercepting previous French gold shipments to Canada.

During the spring of 1697, a French ship, having evaded several British blockades, docked in New Orleans. Under watchful eyes, a large shipment in gold coins was transferred from the vessel into several large rafts tied nearby. The gold, all in the form of French-minted coins, was packed in small, wooden kegs. The kegs were lashed tightly to the rafts with ropes.

A group of hardy voyageurs, about twenty in all and veterans of numerous trapping and exploration campaigns throughout the new world, were in New Orleans to receive the shipment. The men were under orders to transport the gold northward, a distance of approximately two thousand miles, and deliver it to the governor in Montreal. The route was to be up the Mississippi River to the Ohio, on to the Allegheny, and up the Conewango to New York's Chautauqua Lake. Following a short portage to Prendergrast Creek and thence to Lake Erie and Lake Ontario, the party would enter the St. Lawrence River and follow it to Montreal.

Under no circumstances were the voyageurs to allow the gold to be taken by the hated English or their allies, the Seneca Indians.

The trip up the Mississippi River was long and tedious and generally uneventful. Bands of Indians were occasionally spotted along the river banks, but no hostile encounters occurred.

On reaching the Ohio River, the party made camp for about a week near the confluence of the two rivers. Here, they rested and made necessary repairs on the rafts. Finally, they returned to the river, and the next few weeks were spent poling up the Ohio River.

Along the way, the voyageurs stopped at friendly settlements to replenish supplies and rest up from their efforts. Each time they stopped, the gold remained under heavy guard.

At Pittsburgh, the travelers halted for another extended

camp. While visiting with residents of the town, they learned that the Seneca Indians were raiding throughout the countryside, killing and scalping settlers, trappers, and Frenchmen wherever they could find them. More cautiously this time, the voyageurs continued on toward Canada, constantly on the alert for trouble.

By the time they reached the tiny settlement of Warren at the confluence of the Conewango River, the Frenchmen learned that the Seneca were aware of their presence in the area and were planning to attack them a short distance upstream. During the respite at Warren, the voyageurs abandoned the rafts and constructed several stout bark canoes in order to more easily navigate the shallower flow they would soon encounter in these upstream waters.

After consulting maps and discussing their plight with Warren residents, the leader of the voyageurs decided against traveling up the Conewango. Instead, he elected to proceed upstream on the Allegheny in order to avoid the Indians.

After transferring the kegs of gold into the canoes, the Frenchmen set out once again, alternately paddling and scanning the adjacent woods for any sign of hostility. On crossing into the state of New York, the Frenchmen learned that several nearby settlements had recently been attacked by Senecas. The voyageurs had no choice but to continue along the Allegheny to its headwaters, make a long portage overland to the Genesee River, and then try to make their way to Montreal.

The Frenchmen had no sooner made the decision to take an alternate route when they were attacked. With the occupants of the canoes alternately paddling and firing into the horde of Indians following them along the shore, they made slow progress upstream. Over the next several weeks, the voyageurs were attacked eight times; four men were killed and six wounded.

Eventually, the group arrived at a relatively broad flood-plain of the Allegheny River, a location known today as the town of Cloudsport. After camping here for several days, they decided to push on toward the Genesee River. This upper stretch of the Allegheny River was too shallow to accommodate the canoes, so after dividing up the supplies, the Frenchmen loaded their packs and the kegs of gold coins onto their backs and proceeded to hike up the river valley.

The voyageurs had not traveled far when the rear guard warned of approaching Indians. Greatly outnumbered and eager to escape, the Frenchmen decided to lighten their load by burying the gold. Once they escaped from the Indians and achieved the safety of Montreal, they intended to request permission to assemble a force and return for the cached treasure.

The Frenchmen selected a location some distance from the river and near a large rock, a rock described as being as "large as a house." After burying the coin-filled kegs, the leader carved a cross into the face of the rock to mark the site. A crude map of the area was hastily drawn, and the location where the treasure was buried was referred to as the Valley of Borie.

Acting quickly, the voyageurs fled through a series of inter-connecting valleys to the Genesee River. After constructing crude rafts by lashing logs together with strips of leather, they floated out of Pennsylvania and across western New York to Lake Ontario. Weeks later, they finally arrived in Montreal, where they reported to the governor.

Because of ongoing hostilities with the Seneca Indians and the growing threat of the English, the French governor decided against an immediate return to the headwaters of the

Allegheny River to retrieve the gold. As time passed, the issue of the buried gold coins was gradually forgotten as matters of war occupied the minds of the leaders.

When hostilities subsided years later, adventurers who eventually learned of the story of the fortune in buried gold coins traveled to the Allegheny River country in northern Pennsylvania in search of the fabulous cache. None were successful.

A few who have researched the tale have uncovered Seneca references to a large rock near the headwaters of the Allegheny River that has an image of "two crossed sticks" chiseled into it. Historically, the Indians interpreted the sign as one of warning and were careful to avoid the so-called Valley of Borie. When they were asked to guide treasure hunters into the area, the Senecas always refused.

Although many have looked for the buried gold-filled kegs, there is no record that this now famous French treasure cache has ever been found.

Susquehanna Indian Silver Mine

For years, rumors have circulated throughout central Pennsylvania regarding the existence of a lost Indian silver mine located somewhere in what is now the Susquehannock State Forest near Keating. Most people dismissed the stories as only fanciful tales made up by local citizens, but continued research into the matter suggests such a mine may actually exist.

* * *

During the first decades of the 1800s, the small settlement of Keating on the south bank of the Sinnemahoning River attracted a few hardy souls who earned a meager living cutting timber. As the timber business grew in the area, Keating enjoyed periods of prosperity, and life was generally good for its citizens.

In 1835, Samuel Groves arrived at Keating in search of work. He was immediately hired as a logger, but since he had no money, he slept in the woods until he was able to afford better accommodations. Presently, a fellow worker named Burns invited Groves to move into his small cabin.

Early one morning, Burns and Groves were splitting firewood in front of the cabin when they spotted a half-dozen Indians approaching along the trail. The Indians, members of the Susquehanna tribe, approached the two men and asked for permission to draw some drinking water from Burns' well. The logger invited the newcomers to help themselves and told them they were welcome to rest for as long as they wished.

Groves noticed that each of the Indians carried an empty pack. Curious, he asked one of them about their destination. The Indian replied by pointing vaguely toward the north. As Groves started to engage the Indian in conversation, however, the leader of the small party interrupted and signaled it was time to move on. Moments later, hiking single file down the narrow trail, they disappeared around a bend and into the forest.

Exactly one week later, Burns and Groves were smoking their pipes on the front porch of the cabin when the same Indians returned along the trail. Once again they asked for water, and, as before, Burns obliged them.

Before drawing water from the well, the Indians dropped their packs. From the porch, Groves noticed that each of the packs was full and apparently quite heavy.

Weary from their trek, the Indians sat in a circle near the well, engaging in quiet discourse. Presently, one of them approached Burns and asked for permission to camp overnight in the woods nearby. Burns told them they were welcome to remain until they were ready to continue on their journey. Furthermore, he said, he had killed and butchered a large deer the previous day and invited the Indians to join him and Groves that evening for dinner. The Indians agreed.

Following a large meal of roasted deer, onions, and corn, the Indians thanked their hosts and, one by one, drifted off toward the edge of the forest where they had set up their camp.

As Groves watched the Indians wander away toward the campsite, he noted that one of them had left his backpack lying near the well. Curious as to what the Susquehannas were transporting, he decided to look into it. After waiting for over an hour until he was certain the guests were asleep,

179

he quietly approached the pack and untied the straps. Peering inside, he was disappointed to see that it contained what appeared to be nothing more than rocks. Removing one of them, Groves noted that the rock seemed heavier than normal. Curious, he carried it into the cabin to examine it in the light of the lantern. As Groves and Burns closely studied the rock, they discovered it was a piece of silver ore, one of very high quality!

The following morning, Groves was determined to question the Indians about the silver and its source, but after rising and walking out to the crude camp, he found they were gone.

After breakfast, Groves and Burns decided to backtrack the trail down which the Indians came. For over two hours they followed it through the rugged woods but lost it where it crossed an extensive rock outcrop.

During the succeeding weeks, when Groves had the opportunity, he traveled to the nearby settlements of Karthus, Lock Haven, and Williamsport to ask many questions about the Indians and their silver. From citizens and merchants, he learned that, from time to time, members of the Susquehanna tribe came out of the nearby forests with silver ore that they generally traded for weapons and food. Each time, the Indians were questioned about the source of their ore, but they replied only in vague and elusive terms. On several occasions, parties of men attempted to follow the Susquehannas into the woods in the hope of locating the mine from which the silver came, but in every case they lost their trail.

Groves made numerous forays into the forest north of Keating in search of a mine. During some of his searches, he remained gone for two weeks at a time or more as he explored among rock outcrops hoping to find some evidence of ore extraction. He found none, but once, while walking along a well-used trail, he found a large silver nugget. Groves presumed it had been dropped by one of the Indians while returning from the mine.

The more Groves considered the notion that a fortune in silver might lie somewhere in the forest not far away, the more determined he became. Eventually, he quit his job with the timber company and devoted all his time to searching for the ore.

Years passed, and Groves had failed to find any of the Susquehanna Indian silver. In the meantime, he learned of fantastic discoveries of gold far away in the west. Believing he might have better luck there, he packed up and traveled to California, hoping to strike it rich.

Groves had only moderate successes in the California gold fields. He eventually married, settled onto a piece of land in northern California, and raised cattle. Over the years, Groves fathered two sons and his cattle ranch prospered, but he could never stop thinking about the huge silver deposit he believed existed in the forests north of Keating, Pennsylvania. Though he was extremely happy in California, Groves constantly fought the urge to return to the Sinnemahoning River country to try to find the mine.

Finally, in 1875, accompanied by his older son, Samuel Groves returned to Keating. Though it had been over two decades since he left, Groves still recognized many of the landmarks and had no trouble finding his way through the still familiar hills and forests.

For several weeks, Groves and his son remained in the area, hiking and camping throughout most of the region north of Keating near Birch Island Run and Spruce Run. Despite their intensive search, they were unable to find any silver. Finally, they gave up and returned to California.

* * *

In 1885, ten years after Samuel Groves and his son made their final search for the silver he believed existed in the Sinnemahoning River country, the decayed body of an elderly Susquehanna Indian was found in the woods about one mile north of Keating. The dead man's family reported him missing nearly one month earlier, but when asked where the old man may have gone, they refused to answer any more questions.

Ordinarily, the death of an Indian would create only a minor stir among central Pennsylvanians around this time, but this case generated a great deal of excitement for, lying next to the body, searchers found a leather backpack filled with remarkably pure silver ore!

Many who have researched the tales of the lost Susquehanna silver near Keating, Pennsylvania, are convinced the old Indian, estimated to be in his seventies, was returning from the secret mine when his heart failed him. At the time, local citizens grew excited about the possibility of finding silver in the area, and soon the forest was filled with searchers. No mine was found, however.

The search continues today. Researchers have accumulated a number of tales and legends from local Indian tribes, many of them having to do with secret silver mines, but thus far the Indians have remained silent about the locations.

Glossary

- **Bayonet:** A steel blade attached to the muzzle end of a rifle or musket and used in hand-to-hand combat

- **Blockade:** The isolation of a particular area, such as a harbor, by a warring nation by means of warships or troops; a measure taken to prevent the passage of people or supplies

- **Bog:** Wet, spongy, poorly drained ground

- **Bordello:** A building in which prostitutes are available; a brothel

- **Bullion:** Gold or silver fashioned into bars or ingots

- **Cache:** A hiding place; a place for storage; a term often used to indicate the location of buried treasure

- **Carriage:** A horse-drawn vehicle for people to ride in

- **Confluence:** A point where two streams meet and flow together

- **Crucible:** A shallow vessel used for melting metals such as gold and silver

- **Entrepreneur:** One who organizes, manages, and assumes the risks of a business or enterprise

- **Foredeck:** The forepart of the ship's main deck

- **Garret:** A room or unfinished part of a house just under the roof

- **Hasp:** A metal bar hinged at one end and pierced near the other and used with staple, toggle, or padlock to fasten a door or trunk

- **Hoard:** A hidden supply or fund

- **Hummock:** A rounded knoll or hill

- **Ingot:** A mass of metal cast into a convenient shape for storage or transportation to be later processed into another form, such as coins

- **Keg:** A small cask or barrel having a capacity of thirty gallons or less; often used to carry or store treasure

- **Kill:** A narrow, navigable body of water in which there is no noticeable current; similar to a strait—a narrow passageway connecting two larger bodies of water

- **Landslide:** The rapid downward movement of a mass of rock or earth on a slope

- **Marsh:** A tract of soft, wet land usually characterized by grasses or cattails

- **Mint:** A place where coins, metals, or tokens are manufactured

- **Musket:** A heavy, large-caliber, smoothbore shoulder firearm such as a flintlock or matchlock

- **Ore:** A mineral source from which valuable matter is extracted; the raw material that is mined

- **Outcrop:** A projection of bedrock from the surrounding soil or ground

- **Pier:** A structure extending into navigable water for use as a landing place

- **Plantation:** A large single-crop farm

- **Plat:** A survey map of a piece of land

- **Port:** The left side of a ship

- **Quicksand:** A deep mass of loosely consolidated sand mixed with water into which heavy objects readily sink

- **Rivulet:** A small stream or brook

- **Salvor:** One engaged in the business of salvage and recovery for money

- **Seneca:** A tribe of American Indians whose homeland was originally western New York

- **Starboard:** The right side of a ship

- **Tavern:** An establishment where alcoholic beverages are sold to be drunk on the premises

- **Tory:** A seventeenth century royalist outlaw; a member or supporter of a major British political group of the eighteenth and early nineteenth centuries; an American upholding the cause of the British crown against the supporters of colonial independence during the American Revolution

- **Tugboat:** A strongly built, powerful boat used for towing and pushing

- **Voyageur:** A man employed by a fur company to transport goods and men to and from remote stations

Selected References

Carson, Xanthus. "Pennsylvania's Missing Bank Loot," *Treasure World*, June-July, 1969.

Dangerfield, Dan. "French Trove on Treasure Island," *Lost Treasure*, September, 1978.

Duffy, Howard M. "Missing Tory Treasure in Orange County," *Lost Treasure*, November, 1977.

_____. "The Twice-Lost Hudson Gold Mine," *Treasure World*, June-July, 1975.

_____. "Lost Bonanza of Bucks County," *True Treasure*, January-February, 1974.

Getz, Donald E. "Murder Tavern of Fat Patty Cannon," *True Treasure*, September-October, 1972.

Henson, Michael Paul. "Delaware: Loaded With Loot," *Lost Treasure*, January, 1995.

_____. "New York: A State in Dutch," *Lost Treasure*, July, 1995.

_____. "Pennsylvania's Treasures of Intrigue," *Lost Treasure*, May, 1995.

_____. "Braddock's Field of Dreams," *Treasure Cache*, 1995.

_____. "New Jersey's Stockpiles of Treasure," *Lost Treasure*, November, 1994.

_____. "The Mixed Treasures of Maryland," *Lost Treasure*, July, 1994.

_____. "New York: Treasure Sites Worth Investigating," *Lost Treasure*, January, 1993.

_____. "Delaware," *Treasure Cache*, 1993.

_____. "Maryland," *Treasure Cache*, 1993.

_____. "New Jersey Caches," *Lost Treasure*, December, 1991.

_____. "Maryland: The Tale of Braddock's Payroll," *Lost Treasure*, June, 1991.

_____. Personal notes and correspondence collected between 1961 and 1992.

Jecas, Nelson, and Bukowski, Diana C. "Haunted Treasure of the Spy House," *Treasure Search*, Vol. 1, no. 4. 1994.

Ladd, Rex. "Dutch Schultz's Missing $7 Million Cache," *Treasure World*, February-March, 1973.

Loeper, John J. "Treasure of the Doane Brothers," *Lost Treasure*, Winter, 1967.

_____. "Pirate Gold in Pennsylvania," *True Treasure*, Summer, 1967.

Nannetti, Ettore, and Nannetti, Diana. "Eastern Caches," *Lost Treasure*, March, 1944.

_____. "New York's Hermit Caches," *Lost Treasure*, May, 1993.

_____. "New York's Hermit Caches, Part II," *Lost Treasure*, June, 1993.

_____. "New York's Tory Treasures," *Lost Treasure*, April, 1993.

Pallante, Anthony J. "New Jersey Caches of the Pine Robbers," *Lost Treasure*, April, 1996.

Remick, Teddy. "Missing—115 Tons of Silver," *Treasure World*, February-March, 1970.

Voynick, Stephen M. *The Mid-Atlantic Treasure Coast*. Wallingford, Penn.: The Middle Atlantic Press, 1984.

Weinman, Ken. "Secret Silver of the Susquehanna," *Lost Treasure*, June, 1996.

_____. "Strongbox For A Strongarm: Dutch's Missing Money," *Treasure Cache*, 1994 Annual.